DR JEKYLL AND MR HYDE

In seeking to discover his inner self, the brilliant Dr Henry Jekyll discovers a monster. Developing a serum with the intent of separating his good side from his darker impulses, he periodically transforms into Edward Hyde, a brutal creature, free of any conscience. The scientist's strange behaviour is investigated by his friend, the lawyer John Utterson. What follows is a classic thriller, and a terrifying study of the duality of human nature. Also included in this collection are five other classic tales of mystery and horror, from some of the greatest writers of the era.

Books by Sir Arthur Conan Doyle
Published by The House of Ulverscroft:

A STUDY IN SCARLET
THE SIGN OF FOUR
THE ADVENTURES OF SHERLOCK HOLMES
MEMOIRS OF SHERLOCK HOLMES
THE HOUND OF THE BASKERVILLES
THE RETURN OF SHERLOCK HOLMES
THE VALLEY OF FEAR
HIS LAST BOW
THE CASE BOOK OF SHERLOCK HOLMES
THE EXPLOITS OF BRIGADIER GERARD
THE ADVENTURES OF GERARD
THE LOST WORLD
THE POISON BELT

Books by Rudyard Kipling
Published by The House of Ulverscroft:

CAPTAINS COURAGEOUS
THE LIGHT THAT FAILED
KIM
STALKY & CO.
THE JUNGLE BOOK
THE SECOND JUNGLE BOOK

SPECIAL MESSAGE TO READERS

THE ULVERSCROFT FOUNDATION
(registered UK [illegible] 264873)
was established in 1972 to [illegible] funds for research, diagnosis and [illegible] eye diseases. Examples of major [illegible] funded by the Ulverscroft Foundation are:-

- The Children's Eye Unit at Moorfields Eye Hospital, London
- The Ulverscroft Children's Eye Unit at Great Ormond Street Hospital for Sick Children
- Funding research into eye diseases and treatment at the Department of Ophthalmology, University of Leicester
- The Ulverscroft Vision Research Group, Institute of Child Health
- Twin operating theatres at the Western Ophthalmic Hospital, London
- The Chair of Ophthalmology at the Royal Australian College of Ophthalmologists

You can help further the work of the Foundation by making a donation or leaving a legacy. Every contribution is gratefully received. If you would like to help support the Foundation or require further information, please contact:

THE ULVERSCROFT FOUNDATION
The Green, Bradgate Road, Anstey
Leicester LE7 7FU, England
Tel: (0116) 236 4325

website: [illegible]oft.com

Robert Louis Stevenson was born in Edinburgh in 1850. Having no desire to join his family's business of lighthouse engineering, he travelled often and developed his desire to write from a young age. After finishing law school at the age of 25 he decided not to practise, instead pursuing a career in writing, and marrying in 1880 in California. His increasingly failing health after his marriage left him bedridden for several years. However, this allowed him to concentrate on his writing and led to some of his most successful works, including *Treasure Island* in 1883 and *The Strange Case of Dr Jekyll and Mr Hyde* in 1886. By the end of the 1880s he was one of the most popular and widely read authors of the period. He spent the last years of his life in Samoa, where he built a house and settled with his wife and stepchildren. The authors in this collection were all supremely popular and influential in their time, and their works continue to be enjoyed to this day.

ROBERT LOUIS STEVENSON
AND OTHERS

DR JEKYLL AND MR HYDE

AND OTHER TALES

Complete and Unabridged

ULVERSCROFT
Leicester

Dr Jekyll and Mr Hyde — Robert Louis Stevenson
First published in Great Britain in 1886

'Oh, Whistle, and I'll Come to You, My Lad'
— M. R. James
First published in Great Britain in 1904

Lot No. 249 — Sir Arthur Conan Doyle
First published in Great Britain in 1892

A Tough Tussle — Ambrose Bierce
First published in the United States of America in 1891

Lady Wishaw's Hand — Richard Marsh
First published in Great Britain in 1898

The Mark of the Beast — Rudyard Kipling
First published in India in 1890

This Large Print Edition
published 2015

A catalogue record for this book is available from the British Library.

ISBN 978–1–4448–2257–1

Published by
F. A. Thorpe (Publishing)
Anstey, Leicestershire

Set by Words & Graphics Ltd.
Anstey, Leicestershire
Printed and bound in Great Britain by
T. J. International Ltd., Padstow, Cornwall

This book is printed on acid-free paper

Contents

DR JEKYLL AND MR HYDE

Robert Louis Stevenson

Story of the Door

Mr Utterson the lawyer was a man of a rugged countenance, that was never lighted by a smile; cold, scanty and embarrassed in discourse; backward in sentiment; lean, long, dusty, dreary, and yet somehow lovable. At friendly meetings, and when the wine was to his taste, something eminently human beaconed from his eye; something indeed which never found its way into his talk, but which spoke not only in these silent symbols of the after-dinner face, but more often and loudly in the acts of his life. He was austere with himself; drank gin when he was alone, to mortify a taste for vintages; and though he enjoyed the theatre, had not crossed the doors of one for twenty years. But he had an approved tolerance for others; sometimes wondering, almost with envy, at the high pressure of spirits involved in their misdeeds; and in any extremity inclined to help rather than to reprove. 'I incline to Cain's heresy,' he used to say quaintly: 'I let my brother go to the devil in his own way.' In this character it was frequently his fortune to be the last reputable acquaintance and the last good influence in the lives of down-going men. And to such as these, so long as they came about his chambers, he never marked a shade of change in his demeanour.

No doubt the feat was easy to Mr Utterson; for he was undemonstrative at the best, and even his friendships seemed to be founded in a similar catholicity of good-nature. It is the mark of a modest man to accept his friendly circle ready made from the hands of opportunity; and that was the lawyer's way. His friends were those of his own blood, or those whom he had known the longest; his affections, like ivy, were the growth of time, they implied no aptness in the object. Hence, no doubt, the bond that united him to Mr Richard Enfield, his distant kinsman, the well-known man about town. It was a nut to crack for many, what these two could see in each other, or what subject they could find in common. It was reported by those who encountered them in their Sunday walks, that they said nothing, looked singularly dull, and would hail with obvious relief the appearance of a friend. For all that, the two men put the greatest store by these excursions, counted them the chief jewel of each week, and not only set aside occasions of pleasure, but even resisted the calls of business, that they might enjoy them uninterrupted.

It chanced on one of these rambles that their way led them down a by-street in a busy quarter of London. The street was small and what is called quiet, but it drove a thriving trade on the week-days. The inhabitants were all doing well, it seemed, and all emulously hoping to do better still, and laying out the surplus of their gains in coquetry; so that the shop fronts stood along that thoroughfare with an air of invitation, like rows of smiling saleswomen. Even on Sunday, when it veiled its more florid charms and lay comparatively empty of passage, the street shone out in contrast to its dingy neighbourhood, like a fire in a forest; and with its freshly painted shutters, well-polished brasses, and general cleanliness and gaiety of note, instantly caught and pleased the eye of the passenger.

Two doors from one corner, on the left hand going east, the line was broken by the entry of a court; and just at that point, a certain sinister block of building thrust forward its gable on the street. It was two storeys high; showed no window, nothing but a door on the lower storey and a blind forehead of discoloured wall on the upper; and bore in every feature the marks of prolonged and sordid negligence. The door, which was equipped with neither bell nor knocker, was blistered and distained. Tramps slouched into the recess and struck matches on the panels; children kept shop upon the steps; the schoolboy had tried his knife on the mouldings; and for close on a generation no one had appeared to drive away these random visitors or to repair their ravages.

Mr Enfield and the lawyer were on the other side of the by-street; but when they came abreast of the entry, the former lifted up his cane and pointed.

'Did you ever remark that door?' he asked; and when his companion had replied in the affirmative, 'It is connected in my mind,' added he, 'with a very odd story.'

'Indeed!' said Mr Utterson, with a slight change of voice, 'and what was that?'

'Well, it was this way,' returned Mr Enfield: 'I was coming home from some place at the end of the world, about three o'clock of a black winter morning, and my way lay through a part of town where there was literally nothing to be seen but lamps. Street after street, and all the folks asleep — street after street, all lighted up as if for a procession, and all as empty as a church — till at last I got into that state of mind when a man listens and listens and begins to long for the sight of a policeman. All at once,

I saw two figures: one a little man who was stumping along eastward at a good walk, and the other a girl of maybe eight or ten who was running as hard as she was able down a cross-street. Well, sir, the two ran into one another naturally enough at the corner; and then came the horrible part of the thing; for the man trampled calmly over the child's body and left her screaming on the ground. It sounds nothing to hear, but it was hellish to see. It wasn't like a man; it was like some damned Juggernaut. I gave a view-halloa, took to my heels, collared my gentleman, and brought him back to where there was already quite a group about the screaming child. He was perfectly cool and made no resistance, but gave me one look, so ugly that it brought out the sweat on me like running. The people who had turned out were the girl's own family; and pretty soon the doctor, for whom she had been sent, put in his appearance. Well, the child was not much the worse, more frightened, according to the Sawbones; and there you might have supposed would be an end to it. But there was one curious circumstance. I had taken a loathing to my gentleman at first sight. So had the child's family, which was only natural. But the doctor's case was what struck me. He was the usual cut-and-dry apothecary, of no particular age and colour, with a strong Edinburgh accent, and about as emotional as a bagpipe. Well, sir, he was like the rest of us: every time he looked at my prisoner, I saw that Sawbones turned sick and white with the desire to kill him. I knew what was in his mind, just as he knew what was in mine; and killing being out of the question, we did the next best. We told the man we could and would make such a scandal out of this, as should make his name stink from one end of London to the other. If he had any friends or any credit, we undertook that he should lose them. And all the time, as we were pitching it in red hot, we were keeping the women off him as best we could, for they were as wild as harpies. I never saw a circle of such hateful faces; and there was the man in the middle, with a kind of black sneering coolness — frightened too, I could see that — but carrying it off, sir, really like Satan. 'If you choose to make capital out of this accident,' said he, 'I am naturally helpless. No gentleman but wishes to avoid a scene,' says he. 'Name your figure.' Well, we screwed him up to a hundred pounds for the child's family; he would have clearly liked to stick out; but there was something about the lot of us that meant mischief, and at last he struck. The next thing was to get the money; and where do you think he carried us but to that place with the door? — whipped out a key, went in, and presently came back with the matter of ten pounds in gold and a cheque for the balance on Coutts's, drawn payable to bearer, and signed with a name that I can't mention, though it's one of the points of my story, but it was a name at least very well known and often printed. The figure was stiff: but the signature was good for more than that, if it was only genuine. I took the liberty of pointing out to my gentleman that the whole business looked apocryphal; and that a man does not, in real life, walk into a cellar door at four in the morning and come out of it with another man's cheque for close upon a hundred pounds. But he was quite easy and sneering. 'Set your mind at rest,' says he; 'I will stay with you till the banks open, and cash the cheque myself.' So we all set off, the doctor, and the child's father, and our friend and myself, and passed the rest of the night in my chambers; and next day, when we had breakfasted, went in a body to the bank. I gave in the cheque myself, and said I had every reason to believe it was a forgery. Not a bit of it. The cheque was genuine.'

'Tut-tut!' said Mr Utterson.

'I see you feel as I do,' said Mr Enfield. 'Yes, it's a bad story. For my man was a fellow that nobody could have to do with, a really damnable man; and the person that drew the cheque is the very pink of the proprieties, celebrated too, and (what makes it worse) one of your fellows who do what they call good. Blackmail, I suppose; an honest man paying through the nose for some of the capers of his youth. Blackmail House is what I call that place with the door, in consequence. Though even that, you know, is far from explaining all,' he added; and with the words fell into a vein of musing.

From this he was recalled by Mr Utterson asking rather suddenly: 'And you don't know if the drawer of the cheque lives there?'

'A likely place, isn't it?' returned Mr Enfield. 'But I happen to have noticed his address; he lives in some square or other.'

'And you never asked about — the place with the door?' said Mr Utterson.

'No, sir: I had a delicacy,' was the reply. 'I feel very strongly about putting questions; it partakes too much of the style of the day of judgment. You start a question, and it's like starting a stone. You sit quietly on the top of a hill; and away the stone goes, starting others; and presently some bland old bird (the last you would have thought of) is knocked on the head in his own back garden, and the family have to change their name. No, sir, I make it a rule of mine: the more it looks like Queer Street, the less I ask.'

'A very good rule, too,' said the lawyer.

'But I have studied the place for myself,' continued Mr Enfield. 'It seems scarcely a house. There is no other door, and nobody goes in or out of that one, but, once in a great while, the gentleman of my adventure. There are three windows looking on the court on the first floor; none below; the windows are always shut, but they're clean. And then there is a chimney, which is generally smoking; so somebody must live there. And yet it's not so sure; for the buildings are so packed together about that court, that it's hard to say where one ends and another begins.'

The pair walked on again for a while in silence; and then — 'Enfield,' said Mr Utterson, 'that's a good rule of yours.'

'Yes, I think it is,' returned Enfield.

'But for all that,' continued the lawyer, 'there's one point I want to ask: I want to ask the name of that man who walked over the child.'

'Well,' said Mr Enfield, 'I can't see what

harm it would do. It was a man of the name of Hyde.'

'Hm,' said Mr Utterson. 'What sort of a man is he to see?'

'He is not easy to describe. There is something wrong with his appearance; something displeasing, something downright detestable. I never saw a man I so disliked, and yet I scarce know why. He must be deformed somewhere; he gives a strong feeling of deformity, although I couldn't specify the point. He's an extraordinary-looking man, and yet I really can name nothing out of the way. No, sir; I can make no hand of it; I can't describe him. And it's not want of memory; for I declare I can see him this moment.'

Mr Utterson again walked some way in silence, and obviously under a weight of consideration. 'You are sure he used a key?' he inquired at last.

'My dear sir . . . ' began Enfield, surprised out of himself.

'Yes, I know,' said Utterson; 'I know it must seem strange. The fact is, if I do not ask you the name of the other party, it is because I know it already. You see, Richard, your tale has gone home. If you have been inexact in any point, you had better correct it.'

'I think you might have warned me,'

returned the other, with a touch of sullenness. 'But I have been pedantically exact, as you call it. The fellow had a key; and, what's more, he has it still. I saw him use it, not a week ago.'

Mr Utterson sighed deeply, but said never a word; and the young man presently resumed. 'Here is another lesson to say nothing,' said he. 'I am ashamed of my long tongue. Let us make a bargain never to refer to this again.'

'With all my heart,' said the lawyer. 'I shake hands on that, Richard.'

Search for Mr Hyde

That evening Mr Utterson came home to his bachelor house in sombre spirits, and sat down to dinner without relish. It was his custom of a Sunday, when this meal was over, to sit close by the fire, a volume of some dry divinity on his reading-desk, until the clock of the neighbouring church rang out the hour of twelve, when he would go soberly and gratefully to bed. On this night, however, as soon as the cloth was taken away, he took up a candle and went into his business room. There he opened his safe, took from the most private part of it a document endorsed on the envelope as Dr Jekyll's Will, and sat down with a clouded brow to study its contents. The will was holograph; for Mr Utterson, though he took charge of it now that it was made, had refused to lend the least assistance in the making of it; it provided not only that, in case of the decease of Henry Jekyll, M.D., D.C.L., LL.D., F.R.S., &c., all his possessions were to pass into the hands of his 'friend and benefactor Edward Hyde'; but that in case of Dr

Jekyll's 'disappearance or unexplained absence for any period exceeding three calendar months,' the said Edward Hyde should step into the said Henry Jekyll's shoes without further delay, and free from any burthen or obligation, beyond the payment of a few small sums to the members of the doctor's household. This document had long been the lawyer's eyesore. It offended him both as a lawyer and as a lover of the sane and customary sides of life, to whom the fanciful was the immodest. And hitherto it was his ignorance of Mr Hyde that had swelled his indignation; now, by a sudden turn, it was his knowledge. It was already bad enough when the name was but a name of which he could learn no more. It was worse when it began to be clothed upon with detestable attributes; and out of the shifting, insubstantial mists that had so long baffled his eye, there leaped up the sudden, definite presentment of a fiend.

'I thought it was madness,' he said, as he replaced the obnoxious paper in the safe; 'and now I begin to fear it is disgrace.'

With that he blew out his candle, put on a great-coat, and set forth in the direction of Cavendish Square, that citadel of medicine, where his friend, the great Dr Lanyon, had his house and received his crowding patients.

'If any one knows, it will be Lanyon,' he had thought.

The solemn butler knew and welcomed him; he was subjected to no stage of delay, but ushered direct from the door to the dining-room, where Dr Lanyon sat alone over his wine. This was a hearty, healthy, dapper, red-faced gentleman, with a shock of hair prematurely white, and a boisterous and decided manner. At sight of Mr Utterson, he sprang up from his chair and welcomed him with both hands. The geniality, as was the way of the man, was somewhat theatrical to the eye; but it reposed on genuine feeling. For these two were old friends, old mates both at school and college, both thorough respecters of themselves and of each other, and, what does not always follow, men who thoroughly enjoyed each other's company.

After a little rambling talk, the lawyer led up to the subject which so disagreeably preoccupied his mind.

'I suppose, Lanyon,' he said, 'you and I must be the two oldest friends that Henry Jekyll has?'

'I wish the friends were younger,' chuckled Dr Lanyon. 'But I suppose we are. And what of that? I see little of him now.'

'Indeed!' said Utterson. 'I thought you had a bond of common interest.'

'We had,' was his reply. 'But it is more than ten years since Henry Jekyll became too fanciful for me. He began to go wrong, wrong in mind; and though, of course, I continue to take an interest in him for old sake's sake as they say, I see and I have seen devilish little of the man. Such unscientific balderdash,' added the doctor, flushing suddenly purple, 'would have estranged Damon and Pythias.'

This little spirt of temper was somewhat of a relief to Mr Utterson. 'They have only differed on some point of science,' he thought; and being a man of no scientific passions (except in the matter of conveyancing), he even added: 'It is nothing worse than that!' He gave his friend a few seconds to recover his composure, and then approached the question he had come to put.

'Did you ever come across a *protégé* of his — one Hyde?' he asked.

'Hyde?' repeated Lanyon. 'No. Never heard of him. Since my time.'

That was the amount of information that the lawyer carried back with him to the great, dark bed on which he tossed to and fro until the small hours of the morning began to grow large. It was a night of little ease to his toiling mind, toiling in mere darkness and besieged by questions.

Six o'clock struck on the bells of the

church that was so conveniently near to Mr Utterson's dwelling, and still he was digging at the problem. Hitherto it had touched him on the intellectual side alone; but now his imagination also was engaged, or rather enslaved; and as he lay and tossed in the gross darkness of the night and the curtained room, Mr Enfield's tale went by before his mind in a scroll of lighted pictures. He would be aware of the great field of lamps of a nocturnal city; then of the figure of a man walking swiftly; then of a child running from the doctor's; and then these met, and that human Juggernaut trod the child down and passed on regardless of her screams. Or else he would see a room in a rich house, where his friend lay asleep, dreaming and smiling at his dreams; and then the door of that room would be opened, the curtains of the bed plucked apart, the sleeper recalled, and, lo! there would stand by his side a figure to whom power was given, and even at that dead hour he must rise and do its bidding. The figure in these two phases haunted the lawyer all night; and if at any time he dozed over, it was but to see it glide more stealthily through sleeping houses, or move the more swiftly, and still the more swiftly, even to dizziness, through wider labyrinths of lamp-lighted city, and at every street corner crush a child and leave her screaming. And still the figure had no face by which he might know it; even in his dreams it had no face, or one that baffled him and melted before his eyes; and thus it was that there sprang up and grew apace in the lawyer's mind a singularly strong, almost an inordinate, curiosity to behold the features of the real Mr Hyde. If he could but once set eyes on him, he thought the mystery would lighten and perhaps roll altogether away, as was the habit of mysterious things when well examined. He might see a reason for his friend's strange preference or bondage (call it which you please), and even for the startling clauses of the will. And at least it would be a face worth seeing: the face of a man who was without bowels of mercy: a face which had but to show itself to raise up, in the mind of the unimpressionable Enfield, a spirit of enduring hatred.

From that time forward, Mr Utterson began to haunt the door in the by-street of shops. In the morning before office hours, at noon when business was plenty and time scarce, at night under the face of the fogged city moon, by all lights and at all hours of solitude or concourse, the lawyer was to be found on his chosen post.

'If he be Mr Hyde,' he had thought, 'I shall be Mr Seek.'

And at last his patience was rewarded. It was a fine dry night; frost in the air; the streets as clean as a ball-room floor; the lamps, unshaken by any wind, drawing a regular pattern of light and shadow. By ten o'clock, when the shops were closed, the by-street was very solitary, and, in spite of the low growl of London from all round, very silent. Small sounds carried far; domestic sounds out of the houses were clearly audible on either side of the roadway; and the rumour of the approach of any passenger preceded him by a long time. Mr Utterson had been some minutes at his post when he was aware of an odd light footstep drawing near. In the course of his nightly patrols he had long grown accustomed to the quaint effect with which the footfalls of a single person, while he is still a great way off, suddenly spring out distinct from the vast hum and clatter of the city. Yet his attention had never before been so sharply and decisively arrested; and it was with a strong, superstitious prevision of success that he withdrew into the entry of the court.

The steps drew swiftly nearer, and swelled out suddenly louder as they turned the end of the street. The lawyer, looking forth from the entry, could soon see what manner of man he had to deal with. He was small, and very plainly dressed; and the look of him, even at that distance, went somehow strongly against the watcher's inclination. But he made straight for the door, crossing the roadway to save time; and as he came, he drew a key from his pocket, like one approaching home.

Mr Utterson stepped out and touched him on the shoulder as he passed. 'Mr Hyde, I think?'

Mr Hyde shrank back with a hissing intake of the breath. But his fear was only momentary; and though he did not look the lawyer in the face, he answered coolly enough: 'That is my name. What do you want?'

'I see you are going in,' returned the lawyer. 'I am an old friend of Dr Jekyll's — Mr Utterson, of Gaunt Street — you must have heard my name; and meeting you so conveniently, I thought you might admit me.'

'You will not find Dr Jekyll; he is from home,' replied Mr Hyde, blowing in the key. And then suddenly, but still without looking up, 'How did you know me?' he asked.

'On your side,' said Mr Utterson, 'will you do me a favour?'

'With pleasure,' replied the other. 'What shall it be?'

'Will you let me see your face?' asked the lawyer.

Mr Hyde appeared to hesitate; and then, as if upon some sudden reflection, fronted about with an air of defiance; and the pair stared at each other pretty fixedly for a few seconds. 'Now I shall know you again,' said Mr Utterson. 'It may be useful.'

'Yes,' returned Mr Hyde, 'it is as well we have met; and *à propos*, you should have my address.' And he gave a number of a street in Soho.

'Good God!' thought Mr Utterson, 'can he too have been thinking of the will?' But he kept his feelings to himself, and only grunted in acknowledgment of the address.

'And now,' said the other, 'how did you know me?'

'By description,' was the reply.

'Whose description?'

'We have common friends,' said Mr Utterson.

'Common friends!' echoed Mr Hyde, a little hoarsely. 'Who are they?'

'Jekyll, for instance,' said the lawyer.

'He never told you,' cried Mr Hyde, with a flush of anger. 'I did not think you would have lied.'

'Come,' said Mr Utterson, 'that is not fitting language.'

The other snarled aloud into a savage laugh; and the next moment, with extraordinary quickness, he had unlocked the door and disappeared into the house.

The lawyer stood awhile when Mr Hyde had left him, the picture of disquietude. Then he began slowly to mount the street, pausing every step or two, and putting his hand to his brow like a man in mental perplexity. The problem he was thus debating as he walked was one of a class that is rarely solved. Mr Hyde was pale and dwarfish; he gave an impression of deformity without any nameable malformation, he had a displeasing smile, he had borne himself to the lawyer with a sort of murderous mixture of timidity and boldness, and he spoke with a husky, whispering and somewhat broken voice, all these were points against him; but not all of these together could explain the hitherto unknown disgust, loathing and fear with which Mr Utterson regarded him. 'There must be something else,' said the perplexed gentleman. 'There *is* something more, if I could find a name for it. God bless me, the man seems hardly human! Something troglodytic, shall we say? or can it be the old story of Dr Fell? or is it the mere radiance of a foul soul that thus transpires through, and transfigures, its clay continent? The last, I think; for, O my poor old Harry Jekyll, if ever I read Satan's signature upon a face, it is on that of your new friend!'

Round the corner from the by-street there was a square of ancient, handsome houses, now for the most part decayed from their high estate, and let in flats and chambers to all sorts and conditions of men: map-engravers, architects, shady lawyers, and the agents of obscure enterprises. One house, however, second from the corner, was still occupied entire; and at the door of this, which wore a great air of wealth and comfort, though it was now plunged in darkness except for the fan-light, Mr Utterson stopped and knocked. A well-dressed, elderly servant opened the door.

'Is Dr Jekyll at home, Poole?' asked the lawyer.

'I will see, Mr Utterson,' said Poole, admitting the visitor, as he spoke, into a large, low-roofed, comfortable hall, paved with flags, warmed (after the fashion of a country house) by a bright, open fire, and furnished with costly cabinets of oak. 'Will you wait here by the fire, sir? or shall I give you a light in the dining-room?'

'Here, thank you,' said the lawyer; and he

drew near and leaned on the tall fender. This hall, in which he was now left alone, was a pet fancy of his friend the doctor's; and Utterson himself was wont to speak of it as the pleasantest room in London. But tonight there was a shudder in his blood; the face of Hyde sat heavy on his memory; he felt (what was rare with him) a nausea and distaste of life; and in the gloom of his spirits, he seemed to read a menace in the flickering of the firelight on the polished cabinets and the uneasy starting of the shadow on the roof. He was ashamed of his relief when Poole presently returned to announce that Dr Jekyll was gone out.

'I saw Mr Hyde go in by the old dissecting-room door, Poole,' he said. 'Is that right, when Dr Jekyll is from home?'

'Quite right, Mr Utterson, sir,' replied the servant. 'Mr Hyde has a key.'

'Your master seems to repose a great deal of trust in that young man, Poole,' resumed the other, musingly.

'Yes, sir, he do indeed,' said Poole. 'We have all orders to obey him.'

'I do not think I ever met Mr Hyde?' asked Utterson.

'O dear no, sir. He never *dines* here,' replied the butler 'Indeed, we see very little of him on this side of the house; he mostly comes and goes by the laboratory.'

'Well, good-night, Poole.'

'Good-night, Mr Utterson.'

And the lawyer set out homeward with a very heavy heart. 'Poor Harry Jekyll,' he thought, 'my mind misgives me he is in deep waters! He was wild when he was young; a long while ago, to be sure; but in the law of God there is no statute of limitations. Ah, it must be that; the ghost of some old sin, the cancer of some concealed disgrace; punishment coming, *pede claudo*, years after memory has forgotten and self-love condoned the fault.' And the lawyer, scared by the thought, brooded awhile on his own past, groping in all the corners of memory, lest by chance some Jack-in-the-Box of an old iniquity should leap to light there. His past was fairly blameless; few men could read the rolls of their life with less apprehension; yet he was humbled to the dust by the many ill things he had done, and raised up again into a sober and fearful gratitude by the many that he had come so near to doing, yet avoided. And then by a return on his former subject, he conceived a spark of hope. 'This Master Hyde, if he were studied,' thought he, 'must have secrets of his own: black secrets, by the look of him; secrets compared to which poor Jekyll's worst would be like sunshine. Things cannot continue as they are. It turns me cold to think of this creature stealing like a thief to Harry's bedside; poor Harry, what a wakening! And the danger of it! for if this Hyde suspect the existence of the will, he may grow impatient to inherit. Ay I must put my shoulder to the wheel — if Jekyll will but let me,' he added, 'if Jekyll will only let me.' For once more he saw before his mind's eye, as clear as a transparency, the strange clauses of the will.

Dr Jekyll was Quite at Ease

A fortnight later, by excellent good fortune, the doctor gave one of his pleasant dinners to some five or six old cronies, all intelligent reputable men, and all judges of good wine; and Mr Utterson so contrived that he remained behind after the others had departed. This was no new arrangement, but a thing that had befallen many scores of times. Where Utterson was liked, he was liked well. Hosts loved to detain the dry lawyer, when the light-hearted and the loose-tongued had already their foot on the threshold; they liked to sit awhile in his unobtrusive company, practising for solitude, sobering their minds in the man's rich silence, after the expense and strain of gaiety. To this rule Dr Jekyll was no exception; and as he now sat on the opposite side of the fire — a large, well-made, smooth-faced man of fifty, with something of a slyish cast perhaps, but every mark of capacity and kindness — you could see by his looks that he cherished for Mr Utterson a sincere and warm affection.

'I have been wanting to speak to you, Jekyll,' began the latter. 'You know that will of yours?'

A close observer might have gathered that the topic was distasteful; but the doctor carried it off gaily. 'My poor Utterson,' said he, 'you are unfortunate in such a client. I never saw a man so distressed as you were by my will; unless it were that hide-bound pedant, Lanyon, at what he called my scientific heresies. O, I know he's a good fellow — you needn't frown — an excellent fellow, and I always mean to see more of him; but a hide-bound pedant for all that; an ignorant, blatant pedant. I was never more disappointed in any man than Lanyon.'

'You know I never approved of it,' pursued Utterson, ruthlessly disregarding the fresh topic.

'My will? Yes, certainly, I know that,' said the doctor, a trifle sharply. 'You have told me so.'

'Well, I tell you so again,' continued the lawyer. 'I have been learning something of young Hyde.'

The large handsome face of Dr Jekyll grew pale to the very lips, and there came a blackness about his eyes. 'I do not care to hear more,' said he. 'This is a matter I thought we had agreed to drop.'

'What I heard was abominable,' said Utterson.

'It can make no change. You do not understand my position,' returned the doctor, with a certain incoherency of manner. 'I am painfully situated, Utterson; my position is a very strange — a very strange one. It is one of those affairs that cannot be mended by talking.'

'Jekyll,' said Utterson, 'you know me: I am a man to be trusted. Make a clean breast of this in confidence; and I make no doubt I can get you out of it.'

'My good Utterson,' said the doctor, 'this is very good of you, this is downright good of you, and I cannot find words to thank you in. I believe you fully; I would trust you before any man alive, ay, before myself, if I could make the choice; but indeed it isn't what you fancy; it is not so bad as that; and just to put your good heart at rest, I will tell you one thing: the moment I choose, I can be rid of Mr Hyde. I give you my hand upon that; and I thank you again and again; and I will just add one little word, Utterson, that I'm sure you'll take in good part: this is a private matter, and I beg of you to let it sleep.'

Utterson reflected a little, looking in the fire.

'I have no doubt you are perfectly right,' he

said at last, getting to his feet.

'Well, but since we have touched upon this business, and for the last time, I hope,' continued the doctor, 'there is one point I should like you to understand. I have really a very great interest in poor Hyde. I know you have seen him; he told me so; and I fear he was rude. But I do sincerely take a great, a very great interest in that young man; and if I am taken away, Utterson, I wish you to promise me that you will bear with him and get his rights for him. I think you would, if you knew all; and it would be a weight off my mind if you would promise.'

'I can't pretend that I shall ever like him,' said the lawyer.

'I don't ask that,' pleaded Jekyll, laying his hand upon the other's arm; 'I only ask for justice; I only ask you to help him for my sake, when I am no longer here.'

Utterson heaved an irrepressible sigh. 'Well,' said he, 'I promise.'

The Carew Murder Case

Nearly a year later, in the month of October, 18—, London was startled by a crime of singular ferocity, and rendered all the more notable by the high position of the victim. The details were few and startling. A maid-servant living alone in a house not far from the river had gone upstairs to bed about eleven. Although a fog rolled over the city in the small hours, the early part of the night was cloudless, and the lane, which the maid's window overlooked, was brilliantly lit by the full moon. It seems she was romantically given; for she sat down upon her box, which stood immediately under the window, and fell into a dream of musing. Never (she used to say, with streaming tears, when she narrated that experience), never had she felt more at peace with all men or thought more kindly of the world. And as she so sat she became aware of an aged and beautiful gentleman with white hair drawing near along the lane; and advancing to meet him, another and very small gentleman, to whom at first she paid less attention. When they had come within speech (which was just under the maid's eyes) the older man bowed and accosted the other with a very pretty manner of politeness. It did not seem as if the subject of his address were of great importance; indeed, from his pointing, it sometimes appeared as if he were only inquiring his way; but the moon shone on his face as he spoke, and the girl was pleased to watch it, it seemed to breathe such an innocent and old-world kindness of disposition, yet with something high too, as of a well-founded self-content. Presently her eye wandered to the other, and she was surprised to recognise in him a certain Mr Hyde, who had once visited her master, and for whom she had conceived a dislike. He had in his hand a heavy cane, with which he was trifling; but he answered never a word, and seemed to listen with an ill-contained impatience. And then all of a sudden he broke out in a great flame of anger, stamping with his foot, brandishing the cane, and carrying on (as the maid described it) like a madman. The old gentleman took a step back, with the air of one very much surprised and a trifle hurt; and at that Mr Hyde broke out of all bounds, and clubbed him to the earth. And next moment, with ape-like fury, he was trampling his victim under foot, and hailing down a storm of blows, under which the bones were audibly shattered and the body jumped upon the roadway. At the horror of these sights and sounds the maid fainted.

It was two o'clock when she came to herself and called for the police. The murderer was gone long ago; but there lay his victim in the middle of the lane, incredibly mangled. The stick with which the deed had been done, although it was of some rare and very tough and heavy wood, had broken in the middle under the stress of this insensate cruelty; and one splintered half had rolled in the neighbouring gutter — the other, without doubt, had been carried away by the murderer. A purse and a gold watch were found upon the victim; but no cards or papers, except a sealed and stamped envelope, which he had been probably carrying to the post, and which bore the name and address of Mr Utterson.

This was brought to the lawyer the next morning, before he was out of bed; and he had no sooner seen it, and been told the circumstances, than he shot out a solemn lip. 'I shall say nothing till I have seen the body,' said he; 'this may be very serious. Have the kindness to wait while I dress.' And with the same grave countenance he hurried through his breakfast and drove to the police station, whither the body had been carried. As soon as he came into the cell, he nodded.

'Yes,' said he, 'I recognise him. I am sorry to say that this is Sir Danvers Carew.'

'Good God, sir!' exclaimed the officer, 'is it possible?' And the next moment his eye lighted up with professional ambition. 'This will make a deal of noise,' he said. 'And perhaps you can help us to the man.' And he briefly narrated what the maid had seen, and showed the broken stick.

Mr Utterson had already quailed at the name of Hyde; but when the stick was laid before him, he could doubt no longer: broken and battered as it was, he recognised it for one that he had himself presented many years before to Henry Jekyll.

'Is this Mr Hyde a person of small stature?' he inquired.

'Particularly small and particularly wicked-looking, is what the maid calls him,' said the officer.

Mr Utterson reflected; and then, raising his head, 'If you will come with me in my cab,' he said, 'I think I can take you to his house.'

It was by this time about nine in the morning, and the first fog of the season. A great chocolate-coloured pall lowered over heaven, but the wind was continually charging and routing these embattled vapours; so that as the cab crawled from street to street, Mr Utterson beheld a marvellous number of degrees and hues of twilight; for here it would be dark like the back-end of evening; and there would be a glow of a rich, lurid brown, like the light of some strange conflagration; and here, for a moment, the fog would be quite broken up, and a haggard shaft of daylight would glance in between the swirling wreaths. The dismal quarter of Soho seen under these changing glimpses, with its muddy ways, and slatternly passengers, and its lamps, which had never been extinguished or had been kindled afresh to combat this mournful reinvasion of darkness, seemed, in the lawyer's eyes, like a district of some city in a nightmare. The thoughts of his mind, besides, were of the gloomiest dye; and when he glanced at the companion of his drive, he was conscious of some touch of that terror of the law and the law's officers which may at times assail the most honest.

As the cab drew up before the address indicated, the fog lifted a little and showed him a dingy street, a gin palace, a low French eating-house, a shop for the retail of penny numbers and two-penny salads, many ragged children huddled in the doorways, and many women of many different nationalities passing out, key in hand, to have a morning glass; and the next moment the fog settled down again upon that part, as brown as umber, and cut him off from his blackguardly surroundings. This was the home of Henry Jekyll's favourite; of a man who was heir to a quarter of a million sterling.

An ivory-faced and silvery-haired old woman opened the door. She had an evil face, smoothed by hypocrisy; but her manners were excellent. Yes, she said, this was Mr Hyde's, but he was not at home; he had been in that night very late, but had gone away again in less than an hour: there was nothing strange in that; his habits were very irregular, and he was often absent; for instance, it was nearly two months since she had seen him till yesterday.

'Very well then, we wish to see his rooms,' said the lawyer; and when the woman began to declare it was impossible, 'I had better tell you who this person is,' he added. 'This is Inspector Newcomen, of Scotland Yard.'

A flash of odious joy appeared upon the woman's face. 'Ah!' said she, 'he is in trouble! What has he done?'

Mr Utterson and the inspector exchanged glances. 'He don't seem a very popular character,' observed the latter. 'And now, my good woman, just let me and this gentleman have a look about us.'

In the whole extent of the house, which but for the old woman remained otherwise empty, Mr Hyde had only used a couple of rooms; but these were furnished with luxury and good taste. A closet was filled with wine; the plate was of silver, the napery elegant; a good picture hung upon the walls, a gift (as Utterson supposed) from Henry Jekyll, who was much of a connoisseur; and the carpets were of many plies and agreeable in colour. At this moment, however, the rooms bore every mark of having been recently and hurriedly ransacked; clothes lay about the floor, with their pockets inside out; lockfast drawers stood open; and on the hearth there lay a pile of gray ashes, as though many papers had been burned. From these embers the inspector disinterred the butt end of a green cheque book which had resisted the action of the fire; the other half of the stick was found behind the door; and as this clinched his suspicions, the officer declared himself delighted. A visit to the bank, where several thousand pounds were found to be lying to the murderer's credit, completed his gratification.

'You may depend upon it, sir,' he told Mr Utterson: 'I have him in my hand. He must have lost his head, or he never would have left the stick, or, above all, burned the cheque book. Why, money's life to the man. We have nothing to do but wait for him at the bank, and get out the handbills.'

This last, however, was not so easy of accomplishment; for Mr Hyde had numbered few familiars — even the master of the servant-maid had only seen him twice; his family could nowhere be traced; he had never been photographed; and the few who could describe him differed widely, as common observers will. Only on one point were they agreed; and that was the haunting sense of unexpressed deformity with which the fugitive impressed his beholders.

Incident of the Letter

It was late in the afternoon when Mr Utterson found his way to Dr Jekyll's door, where he was at once admitted by Poole, and carried down by the kitchen offices and across a yard which had once been a garden, to the building which was indifferently known as the laboratory or the dissecting-rooms. The doctor had bought the house from the heirs of a celebrated surgeon; and his own tastes being rather chemical than anatomical, had changed the destination of the block at the bottom of the garden. It was the first time that the lawyer had been received in that part of his friend's quarters; and he eyed the dingy windowless structure with curiosity, and gazed round with a distasteful sense of strangeness as he crossed the theatre, once crowded with eager students and now lying gaunt and silent, the tables laden with chemical apparatus, the floor strewn with crates and littered with packing straw, and the light falling dimly through the foggy cupola. At the further end, a flight of stairs mounted to a door covered with red baize; and through this Mr Utterson was at last received into the doctor's cabinet. It was a large room, fitted round with glass presses, furnished, among other things, with a cheval-glass and a business table, and looking out upon the court by three dusty windows barred with iron. The fire burned in the grate; a lamp was set lighted on the chimney-shelf, for even in the houses the fog began to lie thickly; and there, close up to the warmth, sat Dr Jekyll, looking deadly sick. He did not rise to meet his visitor, but held out a cold hand, and bade him welcome in a changed voice.

'And now,' said Mr Utterson, as soon as Poole had left them, 'you have heard the news?'

The doctor shuddered. 'They were crying it in the square,' he said. 'I heard them in my dining-room.'

'One word,' said the lawyer. 'Carew was my client, but so are you; and I want to know what I am doing. You have not been mad enough to hide this fellow?'

'Utterson, I swear to God,' cried the doctor, 'I swear to God I will never set eyes on him again. I bind my honour to you that I am done with him in this world. It is all at an end. And indeed he does not want my help; you do not know him as I do; he is safe, he is quite safe; mark my words, he will never more be heard of.'

The lawyer listened gloomily; he did not like his friend's feverish manner. 'You seem pretty sure of him,' said he; 'and for your sake, I hope you may be right. If it came to a trial, your name might appear.'

'I am quite sure of him,' replied Jekyll; 'I have grounds for certainty that I cannot share with any one. But there is one thing on which you may advise me. I have — I have received a letter; and I am at a loss whether I should show it to the police. I should like to leave it in your hands, Utterson; you would judge wisely, I am sure; I have so great a trust in you.'

'You fear, I suppose, that it might lead to his detection?' asked the lawyer.

'No,' said the other. 'I cannot say that I care what becomes of Hyde; I am quite done with him. I was thinking of my own character, which this hateful business has rather exposed.'

Utterson ruminated awhile; he was surprised at his friend's selfishness, and yet relieved by it. 'Well,' said he, at last, 'let me see the letter.'

The letter was written in an odd, upright hand, and signed 'Edward Hyde'; and it signified, briefly enough, that the writer's benefactor, Dr Jekyll, whom he had long so unworthily repaid for a thousand generosities, need labour under no alarm for his safety, as he had means of escape on which he placed a sure dependence. The lawyer liked this letter well enough: it put a better colour on the intimacy than he had looked for; and he blamed himself for some of his past suspicions.

'Have you the envelope?' he asked.

'I burned it,' replied Jekyll, 'before I thought what I was about. But it bore no postmark. The note was handed in.'

'Shall I keep this and sleep upon it?' asked Utterson.

'I wish you to judge for me entirely,' was the reply. 'I have lost confidence in myself.'

'Well, I shall consider,' returned the lawyer. 'And now one word more: it was Hyde who dictated the terms in your will about that disappearance?'

The doctor seemed seized with a qualm of faintness; he shut his mouth tight and nodded.

'I knew it,' said Utterson. 'He meant to murder you. You have had a fine escape.'

'I have had what is far more to the purpose,' returned the doctor solemnly: 'I have had a lesson — O God, Utterson, what a lesson I have had!' And he covered his face for a moment with his hands.

On his way out, the lawyer stopped and

had a word or two with Poole. 'By the by,' said he, 'there was a letter handed in today: what was the messenger like?' But Poole was positive nothing had come except by post; 'and only circulars by that,' he added.

This news sent off the visitor with his fears renewed. Plainly the letter had come by the laboratory door; possibly, indeed, it had been written in the cabinet; and, if that were so, it must be differently judged, and handled with the more caution. The news-boys, as he went, were crying themselves hoarse along the footways: 'Special edition. Shocking murder of an M.P.' That was the funeral oration of one friend and client; and he could not help a certain apprehension lest the good name of another should be sucked down in the eddy of the scandal. It was, at least, a ticklish decision that he had to make; and, self-reliant as he was by habit, he began to cherish a longing for advice. It was not to be had directly; but perhaps, he thought, it might be fished for.

Presently after, he sat on one side of his own hearth, with Mr Guest, his head clerk, upon the other, and midway between, at a nicely calculated distance from the fire, a bottle of a particular old wine that had long dwelt unsunned in the foundations of his house. The fog still slept on the wing above the drowned city, where the lamps glimmered like carbuncles; and through the muffle and smother of these fallen clouds, the procession of the town's life was still rolling in through the great arteries with a sound as of a mighty wind. But the room was gay with firelight. In the bottle the acids were long ago resolved; the imperial dye had softened with time, as the colour grows richer in stained windows; and the glow of hot autumn afternoons on hillside vineyards was ready to be set free and to disperse the fogs of London. Insensibly the lawyer melted. There was no man from whom he kept fewer secrets than Mr Guest; and he was not always sure that he kept as many as he meant. Guest had often been on business to the doctor's: he knew Poole; he could scarce have failed to hear of Mr Hyde's familiarity about the house; he might draw conclusions: was it not as well, then, that he should see a letter which put that mystery to rights? and, above all, since Guest, being a great student and critic of handwriting, would consider the step natural and obliging? The clerk, besides, was a man of counsel; he would scarce read so strange a document without dropping a remark; and by that remark Mr Utterson might shape his future course.

'This is a sad business about Sir Danvers,' he said.

‘Yes, sir, indeed. It has elicited a great deal of public feeling,’ returned Guest. ‘The man, of course, was mad.’

‘I should like to hear your views on that,’ replied Utterson. ‘I have a document here in his handwriting; it is between ourselves, for I scarce know what to do about it; it is an ugly business at the best. But there it is; quite in your way: a murderer’s autograph.’

Guest’s eyes brightened, and he sat down at once and studied it with passion. ‘No, sir,’ he said; ‘not mad; but it is an odd hand.’

‘And by all accounts a very odd writer,’ added the lawyer.

Just then the servant entered with a note.

‘Is that from Dr Jekyll, sir?’ inquired the clerk. ‘I thought I knew the writing. Anything private, Mr Utterson?’

‘Only an invitation to dinner. Why? do you want to see it?’

‘One moment. I thank you, sir’; and the clerk laid the two sheets of paper alongside and sedulously compared their contents. ‘Thank you, sir,’ he said at last, returning both; ‘it’s a very interesting autograph.’

There was a pause, during which Mr Utterson struggled with himself. ‘Why did you compare them, Guest?’ he inquired suddenly.

‘Well, sir,’ returned the clerk, ‘there’s a

rather singular resemblance; the two hands are in many points identical; only differently sloped.'

'Rather quaint,' said Utterson.

'It is, as you say, rather quaint,' returned Guest.

'I wouldn't speak of this note, you know,' said the master.

'No, sir,' said the clerk. 'I understand.'

But no sooner was Mr Utterson alone that night than he locked the note into his safe, where it reposed from that time forward. 'What!' he thought. 'Henry Jekyll forge for a murderer!' And his blood ran cold in his veins.

Remarkable Incident of Dr Lanyon

Time ran on; thousands of pounds were offered in reward, for the death of Sir Danvers was resented as a public injury; but Mr Hyde had disappeared out of the ken of the police as though he had never existed. Much of his past was unearthed, indeed, and all disreputable: tales came out of the man's cruelty, at once so callous and violent, of his vile life, of his strange associates, of the hatred that seemed to have surrounded his career; but of his present whereabouts, not a whisper. From the time he had left the house in Soho on the morning of the murder, he was simply blotted out; and gradually, as time drew on, Mr Utterson began to recover from the hotness of his alarm, and to grow more at quiet with himself. The death of Sir Danvers was, to his way of thinking, more than paid for by the disappearance of Mr Hyde. Now that that evil influence had been withdrawn, a new life began for Dr Jekyll. He came out of his seclusion, renewed relations with his friends, became once more their familiar guest and entertainer; and whilst he had always been known for charities, he was now no less distinguished for religion. He was busy, he was much in the open air, he did good; his face seemed to open and brighten, as if with an inward consciousness of service; and for more than two months the doctor was at peace.

On the 8th of January Utterson had dined at the doctor's with a small party; Lanyon had been there; and the face of the host had looked from one to the other as in the old days when the trio were inseparable friends. On the 12th, and again on the 14th, the door was shut against the lawyer. 'The doctor was confined to the house,' Poole said, 'and saw no one.' On the 15th he tried again, and was again refused; and having now been used for the last two months to see his friend almost daily, he found this return of solitude to weigh upon his spirits. The fifth night he had in Guest to dine with him; and the sixth he betook himself to Dr Lanyon's.

There at least he was not denied admittance; but when he came in, he was shocked at the change which had taken place in the doctor's appearance. He had his death-warrant written legibly upon his face. The rosy man had grown pale; his flesh had fallen away; he was visibly balder and older;

and yet it was not so much these tokens of a swift physical decay that arrested the lawyer's notice, as a look in the eye and quality of manner that seemed to testify to some deep-seated terror of the mind. It was unlikely that the doctor should fear death; and yet that was what Utterson was tempted to suspect. 'Yes,' he thought; 'he is a doctor, he must know his own state and that his days are counted; and the knowledge is more than he can bear.' And yet when Utterson remarked on his ill looks, it was with an air of great firmness that Lanyon declared himself a doomed man.

'I have had a shock,' he said, 'and I shall never recover. It is a question of weeks. Well, life has been pleasant; I liked it; yes, sir, I used to like it. I sometimes think if we knew all, we should be more glad to get away.'

'Jekyll is ill, too,' observed Utterson. 'Have you seen him?'

But Lanyon's face changed, and he held up a trembling hand. 'I wish to see or hear no more of Dr Jekyll,' he said, in a loud, unsteady voice. 'I am quite done with that person; and I beg that you will spare me any allusion to one whom I regard as dead.'

'Tut, tut!' said Mr Utterson; and then, after a considerable pause, 'Can't I do anything?' he inquired. 'We are three very old friends,

Lanyon; we shall not live to make others.'

'Nothing can be done,' returned Lanyon; 'ask himself.'

'He will not see me,' said the lawyer.

'I am not surprised at that,' was the reply. 'Some day, Utterson, after I am dead, you may perhaps come to learn the right and wrong of this. I cannot tell you. And in the meantime, if you can sit and talk with me of other things, for God's sake, stay and do so; but if you cannot keep clear of this accursed topic, then, in God's name, go, for I cannot bear it.'

As soon as he got home, Utterson sat down and wrote to Jekyll, complaining of his exclusion from the house, and asking the cause of this unhappy break with Lanyon; and the next day brought him a long answer, often very pathetically worded, and sometimes darkly mysterious in drift. The quarrel with Lanyon was incurable. 'I do not blame our old friend,' Jekyll wrote, 'but I share his view that we must never meet. I mean from henceforth to lead a life of extreme seclusion; you must not be surprised, nor must you doubt my friendship, if my door is often shut even to you. You must suffer me to go my own dark way. I have brought on myself a punishment and a danger that I cannot name. If I am the chief of sinners, I am the chief of sufferers also. I could not think that this earth contained a place for sufferings and terrors so unmanning; and you can do but one thing, Utterson, to lighten this destiny, and that is to respect my silence.' Utterson was amazed; the dark influence of Hyde had been withdrawn, the doctor had returned to his old tasks and amities; a week ago, the prospect had smiled with every promise of a cheerful and an honoured age; and now in a moment, friendship and peace of mind and the whole tenor of his life were wrecked. So great and unprepared a change pointed to madness; but in view of Lanyon's manner and words, there must lie for it some deeper ground.

A week afterwards Dr Lanyon took to his bed, and in something less than a fortnight he was dead. The night after the funeral, at which he had been sadly affected, Utterson locked the door of his business room, and sitting there by the light of a melancholy candle, drew out and set before him an envelope addressed by the hand and sealed with the seal of his dead friend. 'PRIVATE: for the hands of J. G. Utterson ALONE, and in case of his predecease *to be destroyed unread*,' so it was emphatically superscribed; and the lawyer dreaded to behold the contents. 'I have buried one friend today,' he thought: 'what if this should cost me another?' And then he condemned the fear as a disloyalty, and broke the seal. Within there was another enclosure, likewise sealed, and marked upon the cover as 'not to be opened till the death or disappearance of Dr Henry Jekyll.' Utterson could not trust his eyes. Yes, it was disappearance; here again, as in the mad will, which he had long ago restored to its author, here again were the idea of a disappearance and the name of Henry Jekyll bracketed. But in the will, that idea had sprung from the sinister suggestion of the man Hyde; it was set there with a purpose all too plain and horrible. Written by the hand of Lanyon, what should it mean? A great curiosity came to the trustee, to disregard the prohibition and dive at once to the bottom of these mysteries; but professional honour and faith to his dead friend were stringent obligations; and the packet slept in the inmost corner of his private safe.

It is one thing to mortify curiosity, another to conquer it; and it may be doubted if, from that day forth, Utterson desired the society of his surviving friend with the same eagerness. He thought of him kindly; but his thoughts were disquieted and fearful. He went to call indeed; but he was perhaps relieved to be denied admittance; perhaps, in his heart, he preferred to speak with Poole upon the doorstep, and surrounded by the air and sounds of the open city, rather than to be admitted into that house of voluntary bondage, and to sit and speak with its inscrutable recluse. Poole had, indeed, no very pleasant news to communicate. The doctor, it appeared, now more than ever confined himself to the cabinet over the laboratory, where he would sometimes even sleep: he was out of spirits, he had grown very silent, he did not read; it seemed as if he had something on his mind. Utterson became so used to the unvarying character of these reports, that he fell off little by little in the frequency of his visits.

Incident at the Window

It chanced on Sunday, when Mr Utterson was on his usual walk with Mr Enfield, that their way lay once again through the by-street; and that when they came in front of the door, both stopped to gaze on it.

'Well,' said Enfield, 'that story's at an end, at least. We shall never see more of Mr Hyde.'

'I hope not,' said Utterson. 'Did I ever tell you that I once saw him, and shared your feeling of repulsion?'

'It was impossible to do the one without the other,' returned Enfield. 'And, by the way, what an ass you must have thought me, not to know that this was a back way to Dr Jekyll's! It was partly your own fault that I found it out even when I did.'

'So you found it out, did you?' said Utterson. 'But if that be so, we may step into the court and take a look at the windows. To tell you the truth, I am uneasy about poor Jekyll; and even outside, I feel as if the presence of a friend might do him good.'

The court was very cool and a little damp, and full of premature twilight, although the sky, high up overhead, was still bright with sunset. The middle one of the three windows was half-way open; and sitting close beside it, taking the air with an infinite sadness of mien, like some disconsolate prisoner, Utterson saw Dr Jekyll.

'What! Jekyll!' he cried. 'I trust you are better.'

'I am very low, Utterson,' replied the doctor drearily; 'very low. It will not last long, thank God.'

'You stay too much indoors,' said the lawyer. 'You should be out, whipping up the circulation, like Mr Enfield and me. (This is my cousin — Mr Enfield — Dr Jekyll.) Come, now; get your hat, and take a quick turn with us.'

'You are very good,' sighed the other. 'I should like to very much; but no, no, no; it is quite impossible; I dare not. But indeed, Utterson, I am very glad to see you; this is really a great pleasure. I would ask you and Mr Enfield up, but the place is really not fit.'

'Why then,' said the lawyer, good-naturedly, 'the best thing we can do is to stay down here, and speak with you from where we are.'

'That is just what I was about to venture to propose,' returned the doctor, with a smile. But the words were hardly uttered, before the smile was struck out of his face and succeeded by an expression of such abject terror and despair, as froze the very blood of the two gentlemen below. They saw it but for a glimpse, for the window was instantly thrust down; but that glimpse had been sufficient, and they turned and left the court without a word. In silence, too, they traversed the by-street; and it was not until they had come into a neighbouring thoroughfare, where even upon a Sunday there were still some stirrings of life, that Mr Utterson at last turned and looked at his companion. They were both pale; and there was an answering horror in their eyes.

'God forgive us! God forgive us!' said Mr Utterson.

But Mr Enfield only nodded his head very seriously, and walked on once more in silence.

The Last Night

Mr Utterson was sitting by his fireside one evening after dinner, when he was surprised to receive a visit from Poole.

'Bless me, Poole, what brings you here?' he cried; and then, taking a second look at him, 'What ails you?' he added; 'is the doctor ill?'

'Mr Utterson,' said the man, 'there is something wrong.'

'Take a seat, and here is a glass of wine for you,' said the lawyer. 'Now, take your time, and tell me plainly what you want.'

'You know the doctor's ways, sir,' replied Poole, 'and how he shuts himself up. Well, he's shut up again in the cabinet; and I don't like it, sir — I wish I may die if I like it. Mr Utterson, sir, I'm afraid.'

'Now, my good man,' said the lawyer, 'be explicit. What are you afraid of?'

'I've been afraid for about a week,' returned Poole, doggedly disregarding the question; 'and I can bear it no more.'

The man's appearance amply bore out his words; his manner was altered for the worse; and except for the moment when he had first announced his terror, he had not once looked the lawyer in the face. Even now, he sat with the glass of wine untasted on his knee, and his eyes directed to a corner of the floor. 'I can bear it no more,' he repeated.

'Come,' said the lawyer, 'I see you have some good reason, Poole; I see there is something seriously amiss. Try to tell me what it is.'

'I think there's been foul play,' said Poole, hoarsely.

'Foul play!' cried the lawyer, a good deal frightened, and rather inclined to be irritated in consequence. 'What foul play? What does the man mean?'

'I daren't say, sir,' was the answer; 'but will you come along with me and see for yourself?'

Mr Utterson's only answer was to rise and get his hat and great-coat; but he observed with wonder the greatness of the relief that appeared upon the butler's face, and perhaps with no less, that the wine was still untasted when he set it down to follow.

It was a wild, cold, seasonable night of March, with a pale moon, lying on her back as though the wind had tilted her, and a flying wrack of the most diaphanous and lawny texture. The wind made talking difficult, and flecked the blood into the face. It seemed to have swept the streets unusually bare of passengers, besides; for Mr Utterson thought he had never seen that part of London so deserted. He could have wished it otherwise; never in his life had he been conscious of so sharp a wish to see and touch his fellow-creatures; for, struggle as he might, there was borne in upon his mind a crushing anticipation of calamity. The square, when they got there, was all full of wind and dust, and the thin trees in the garden were lashing themselves along the railing. Poole, who had kept all the way a pace or two ahead, now pulled up in the middle of the pavement, and in spite of the biting weather, took off his hat and mopped his brow with a red pocket-handkerchief. But for all the hurry of his coming, these were not the dews of exertion that he wiped away, but the moisture of some strangling anguish; for his face was white, and his voice, when he spoke, harsh and broken.

'Well, sir,' he said, 'here we are, and God grant there be nothing wrong.'

'Amen, Poole,' said the lawyer.

Thereupon the servant knocked in a very guarded manner; the door was opened on the chain; and a voice asked from within, 'Is that you, Poole?'

'It's all right,' said Poole. 'Open the door.'

The hall, when they entered it, was brightly lighted up; the fire was built high; and about the hearth the whole of the servants, men and women, stood huddled together like a flock of sheep. At the sight of Mr Utterson, the housemaid broke into hysterical whimpering; and the cook, crying out, 'Bless God! it's Mr Utterson,' ran forward as if to take him in her arms.

'What, what? Are you all here?' said the lawyer, peevishly. 'Very irregular, very unseemly: your master would be far from pleased.'

'They're all afraid,' said Poole.

Blank silence followed, no one protesting; only the maid lifted up her voice, and now wept loudly.

'Hold your tongue!' Poole said to her, with a ferocity of accent that testified to his own jangled nerves; and indeed when the girl had so suddenly raised the note of her lamentation, they had all started and turned towards the inner door with faces of dreadful expectation. 'And now,' continued the butler, addressing the knife-boy, 'reach me a candle, and we'll get this through hands at once.' And then he begged Mr Utterson to follow him, and led the way to the back garden.

'Now, sir,' said he, 'you come as gently as you can. I want you to hear, and I don't want you to be heard. And see here, sir, if by any chance he was to ask you in, don't go.'

Mr Utterson's nerves, at this unlooked-for

termination, gave a jerk that nearly threw him from his balance; but he re-collected his courage, and followed the butler into the laboratory building and through the surgical theatre, with its lumber of crates and bottles, to the foot of the stair. Here Poole motioned him to stand on one side and listen; while he himself, setting down the candle and making a great and obvious call on his resolution, mounted the steps, and knocked with a somewhat uncertain hand on the red baize of the cabinet door.

'Mr Utterson, sir, asking to see you,' he called; and even as he did so, once more violently signed to the lawyer to give ear.

A voice answered from within: 'Tell him I cannot see any one,' it said, complainingly.

'Thank you, sir,' said Poole, with a note of something like triumph in his voice; and taking up his candle, he led Mr Utterson back across the yard and into the great kitchen, where the fire was out and the beetles were leaping on the floor.

'Sir,' he said, looking Mr Utterson in the eyes, 'was that my master's voice?'

'It seems much changed,' replied the lawyer, very pale, but giving look for look.

'Changed? Well, yes, I think so,' said the butler. 'Have I been twenty years in this man's house, to be deceived about his voice?

No, sir; master's made away with; he was made away with eight days ago, when we heard him cry out upon the name of God; and *who's* in there instead of him, and *why* it stays there, is a thing that cries to Heaven, Mr Utterson!'

'This is a very strange tale, Poole; this is rather a wild tale, my man,' said Mr Utterson, biting his finger. 'Suppose it were as you suppose, supposing Dr Jekyll to have been — well, murdered, what could induce the murderer to stay? That won't hold water; it doesn't commend itself to reason.'

'Well, Mr Utterson, you are a hard man to satisfy, but I'll do it yet,' said Poole. 'All this last week (you must know), him, or it, or whatever it is that lives in that cabinet, has been crying night and day for some sort of medicine and cannot get it to his mind. It was sometimes his way — the master's, that is — to write his orders on a sheet of paper and throw it on the stair. We've had nothing else this week back; nothing but papers, and a closed door, and the very meals left there to be smuggled in when nobody was looking. Well, sir, every day, ay, and twice and thrice in the same day, there have been orders and complaints, and I have been sent flying to all the wholesale chemists in town. Every time I brought the stuff back, there would be another paper telling me to return it, because it was not pure, and another order to a different firm. This drug is wanted bitter bad, sir, whatever for.'

'Have you any of these papers?' asked Mr Utterson.

Poole felt in his pocket and handed out a crumpled note, which the lawyer, bending nearer to the candle, carefully examined. Its contents ran thus: 'Dr Jekyll presents his compliments to Messrs. Maw. He assures them that their last sample is impure and quite useless for his present purpose. In the year 18—, Dr J. purchased a somewhat large quantity from Messrs. M. He now begs them to search with the most sedulous care, and should any of the same quality be left, to forward it to him at once. Expense is no consideration. The importance of this to Dr J. can hardly be exaggerated.' So far the letter had run composedly enough; but here, with a sudden splutter of the pen, the writer's emotion had broken loose. 'For God's sake,' he had added, 'find me some of the old.'

'This is a strange note,' said Mr Utterson; and then sharply, 'How do you come to have it open?'

'The man at Maw's was main angry, sir, and he threw it back to me like so much dirt,' returned Poole.

'This is unquestionably the doctor's hand, do you know?' resumed the lawyer.

'I thought it looked like it,' said the servant, rather sulkily; and then, with another voice, 'But what matters hand-of-write?' he said. 'I've seen him!'

'Seen him?' repeated Mr Utterson. 'Well?'

'That's it!' said Poole. 'It was this way. I came suddenly into the theatre from the garden. It seems he had slipped out to look for this drug, or whatever it is; for the cabinet door was open, and there he was at the far end of the room, digging among the crates. He looked up when I came in, gave a kind of cry, and whipped upstairs into the cabinet. It was but for one minute that I saw him, but the hair stood upon my head like quills. Sir, if that was my master, why had he a mask upon his face? If it was my master, why did he cry out like a rat and run from me? I have served him long enough. And then . . . ' the man paused, and passed his hand over his face.

'These are all very strange circumstances,' said Mr Utterson, 'but I think I begin to see daylight. Your master, Poole, is plainly seized with one of those maladies that both torture and deform the sufferer; hence, for aught I know, the alteration of his voice; hence the mask and his avoidance of his friends; hence his eagerness to find this drug, by means of which the poor soul retains some hope of ultimate recovery — God grant that he be not deceived! There is my explanation; it is sad enough, Poole, ay, and appalling to consider; but it is plain and natural, hangs well together, and delivers us from all exorbitant alarms.'

'Sir,' said the butler, turning to a sort of mottled pallor, 'that thing was not my master, and there's the truth. My master' — here he looked round him, and began to whisper — 'is a tall fine build of a man, and this was more of a dwarf.' Utterson attempted to protest. 'O, sir,' cried Poole, 'do you think I do not know my master after twenty years? do you think I do not know where his head comes to in the cabinet door, where I saw him every morning of my life? No, sir, that thing in the mask was never Dr Jekyll — God knows what it was, but it was never Dr Jekyll; and it is the belief of my heart that there was murder done.'

'Poole,' replied the lawyer, 'if you say that, it will become my duty to make certain. Much as I desire to spare your master's feelings, much as I am puzzled about this note, which seems to prove him to be still alive, I shall consider it my duty to break in that door.'

'Ah, Mr Utterson, that's talking!' cried the butler.

'And now comes the second question,' resumed Utterson: 'Who is going to do it?'

'Why, you and me, sir,' was the undaunted reply.

'That is very well said,' returned the lawyer; 'and whatever comes of it, I shall make it my business to see you are no loser.'

'There is an axe in the theatre,' continued Poole; 'and you might take the kitchen poker for yourself.'

The lawyer took that rude but weighty instrument into his hand, and balanced it. 'Do you know, Poole,' he said, looking up, 'that you and I are about to place ourselves in a position of some peril?'

'You may say so, sir, indeed,' returned the butler.

'It is well, then, that we should be frank,' said the other. 'We both think more than we have said; let us make a clean breast. This masked figure that you saw, did you recognise it?'

'Well, sir, it went so quick, and the creature was so doubled up, that I could hardly swear to that,' was the answer. 'But if you mean, was it Mr Hyde? — why, yes, I think it was! You see, it was much of the same bigness; and it had the same quick light way with it; and then who else could have got in by the laboratory door? You have not forgot, sir, that at the time of the murder he had still the key with him? But that's not all. I don't know, Mr Utterson, if ever you met this Mr Hyde?'

'Yes,' said the lawyer, 'I once spoke with him.'

'Then you must know, as well as the rest of us, that there was something queer about that gentleman — something that gave a man a turn — I don't know rightly how to say it, sir, beyond this: that you felt it in your marrow — kind of cold and thin.'

'I own I felt something of what you describe,' said Mr Utterson.

'Quite so, sir,' returned Poole. 'Well, when that masked thing like a monkey jumped from among the chemicals and whipped into the cabinet, it went down my spine like ice. O, I know it's not evidence, Mr Utterson; I'm book-learned enough for that; but a man has his feelings; and I give you my bible-word it was Mr Hyde!'

'Ay, ay,' said the lawyer. 'My fears incline to the same point. Evil, I fear, founded — evil was sure to come — of that connection. Ay, truly, I believe you; I believe poor Harry is killed; and I believe his murderer (for what purpose, God alone can tell) is still lurking in his victim's room. Well, let our name be vengeance. Call Bradshaw.'

The footman came at the summons, very

white and nervous.

'Pull yourself together, Bradshaw,' said the lawyer. 'This suspense, I know, is telling upon all of you; but it is now our intention to make an end of it. Poole, here, and I are going to force our way into the cabinet. If all is well, my shoulders are broad enough to bear the blame. Meanwhile, lest anything should really be amiss, or any malefactor seek to escape by the back, you and the boy must go round the corner with a pair of good sticks, and take your post at the laboratory door. We give you ten minutes to get to your stations.'

As Bradshaw left, the lawyer looked at his watch. 'And now, Poole, let us get to ours,' he said; and taking the poker under his arm, he led the way into the yard. The scud had banked over the moon, and it was now quite dark. The wind, which only broke in puffs and draughts into that deep well of building, tossed the light of the candle to and fro about their steps, until they came into the shelter of the theatre, where they sat down silently to wait. London hummed solemnly all around; but nearer at hand, the stillness was only broken by the sound of a footfall moving to and fro along the cabinet floor.

'So it will walk all day, sir,' whispered Poole; 'ay, and the better part of the night. Only when a new sample comes from the chemist, there's a bit of a break. Ah, it's an ill conscience that's such an enemy to rest! Ah, sir, there's blood foully shed in every step of it! But hark again, a little closer — put your heart in your ears, Mr Utterson, and tell me, is that the doctor's foot?'

The steps fell lightly and oddly, with a certain swing, for all they went so slowly; it was different indeed from the heavy creaking tread of Henry Jekyll. Utterson sighed. 'Is there never anything else?' he asked.

Poole nodded. 'Once,' he said. 'Once I heard it weeping!'

'Weeping? how that?' said the lawyer, conscious of a sudden chill of horror.

'Weeping like a woman or a lost soul,' said the butler. 'I came away with that upon my heart, that I could have wept too.'

But now the ten minutes drew to an end. Poole disinterred the axe from under a stack of packing straw; the candle was set upon the nearest table to light them to the attack; and they drew near with bated breath to where that patient foot was still going up and down, up and down in the quiet of the night.

'Jekyll,' cried Utterson, with a loud voice, 'I demand to see you.' He paused a moment, but there came no reply. 'I give you fair warning, our suspicions are aroused, and I must and shall see you,' he resumed; 'if not by fair means, then by foul — if not of your consent, then by brute force!'

'Utterson,' said the voice, 'for God's sake, have mercy!'

'Ah, that's not Jekyll's voice — it's Hyde's!' cried Utterson. 'Down with the door, Poole!'

Poole swung the axe over his shoulder; the blow shook the building, and the red baize door leaped against the lock and hinges. A dismal screech, as of mere animal terror, rang from the cabinet. Up went the axe again, and again the panels crashed and the frame bounded; four times the blow fell; but the wood was tough and the fittings were of excellent workmanship; and it was not until the fifth that the lock burst in sunder, and the wreck of the door fell inwards on the carpet.

The besiegers, appalled by their own riot and the stillness that had succeeded, stood back a little and peered in. There lay the cabinet before their eyes in the quiet lamplight, a good fire glowing and chattering on the hearth, the kettle singing its thin strain, a drawer or two open, papers neatly set forth on the business table, and nearer the fire, the things laid out for tea; the quietest room, you would have said, and, but for the glazed presses full of chemicals, the most commonplace that night in London.

Right in the midst there lay the body of a man sorely contorted and still twitching. They drew near on tiptoe, turned it on its back, and beheld the face of Edward Hyde. He was dressed in clothes far too large for him, clothes of the doctor's bigness; the cords of his face still moved with a semblance of life, but life was quite gone; and by the crushed phial in the hand and the strong smell of kernels that hung upon the air, Utterson knew that he was looking on the body of a self-destroyer.

'We have come too late,' he said sternly, 'whether to save or punish. Hyde is gone to his account; and it only remains for us to find the body of your master.'

The far greater proportion of the building was occupied by the theatre, which filled almost the whole ground storey, and was lighted from above, and by the cabinet, which formed an upper storey at one end and looked upon the court. A corridor joined the theatre to the door on the by-street; and with this, the cabinet communicated separately by a second flight of stairs. There were besides a few dark closets and a spacious cellar. All these they now thoroughly examined. Each closet needed but a glance, for all were empty, and all, by the dust that fell from their doors, had stood long unopened. The cellar, indeed, was filled with crazy lumber, mostly dating from the times of the surgeon who was Jekyll's predecessor; but even as they opened the door, they were advertised of the uselessness of further search by the fall of a perfect mat of cobweb which had for years sealed up the entrance. Nowhere was there any trace of Henry Jekyll, dead or alive.

Poole stamped on the flags of the corridor. 'He must be buried here,' he said, hearkening to the sound.

'Or he may have fled,' said Utterson, and he turned to examine the door in the by-street. It was locked; and lying near by on the flags, they found the key, already stained with rust.

'This does not look like use,' observed the lawyer.

'Use!' echoed Poole. 'Do you not see, sir, it is broken? much as if a man had stamped on it.'

'Ah,' continued Utterson, 'and the fractures, too, are rusty.' The two men looked at each other with a scare. 'This is beyond me, Poole,' said the lawyer. 'Let us go back to the cabinet.'

They mounted the stair in silence, and still, with an occasional awestruck glance at the dead body, proceeded more thoroughly to examine the contents of the cabinet. At one table there were traces of chemical work, various measured heaps of some white salt being laid on glass saucers, as though for an experiment in which the unhappy man had been prevented.

'That is the same drug that I was always bringing him,' said Poole; and even as he spoke, the kettle with a startling noise boiled over.

This brought them to the fireside, where the easy chair was drawn cosily up, and the tea things stood ready to the sitter's elbow, the very sugar in the cup. There were several books on a shelf; one lay beside the tea things open, and Utterson was amazed to find it a copy of a pious work for which Jekyll had several times expressed a great esteem, annotated, in his own hand, with startling blasphemies.

Next, in the course of their review of the chamber, the searchers came to the cheval-glass, into whose depth they looked with an involuntary horror. But it was so turned as to show them nothing but the rosy glow playing on the roof, the fire sparkling in a hundred repetitions along the glazed front of the presses, and their own pale and fearful countenances stooping to look in.

'This glass has seen some strange things, sir,' whispered Poole.

'And surely none stranger than itself,' echoed the lawyer, in the same tone. 'For what did Jekyll' — he caught himself up at the word with a start, and then conquering the weakness — 'what could Jekyll want with it?' he said.

'You may say that!' said Poole.

Next they turned to the business table. On the desk, among the neat array of papers, a large envelope was uppermost, and bore, in the doctor's hand, the name of Mr Utterson. The lawyer unsealed it, and several enclosures fell to the floor. The first was a will, drawn in the same eccentric terms as the one which he had returned six months before, to serve as a testament in case of death and as a deed of gift in case of disappearance; but in place of the name of Edward Hyde, the lawyer, with indescribable amazement, read the name of Gabriel John Utterson. He looked at Poole, and then back at the papers, and last of all at the dead malefactor stretched upon the carpet.

'My head goes round,' he said. 'He has been all these days in possession; he had no cause to like me; he must have raged to see himself displaced; and he has not destroyed this document.'

He caught the next paper; it was a brief note in the doctor's hand, and dated at the top. 'O Poole!' the lawyer cried, 'he was alive and here this day. He cannot have been disposed of in so short a space; he must be still alive, he must have fled! And then, why fled? and how? and in that case can we venture to declare this suicide? O, we must be careful. I foresee that we may yet involve your master in some dire catastrophe.'

'Why don't you read it, sir?' asked Poole.

'Because I fear,' replied the lawyer, solemnly. 'God grant I have no cause for it!' And with that he brought the paper to his eye, and read as follows:

> My dear Utterson, — When this shall fall into your hands I shall have disappeared under what circumstances I have not the penetration to foresee; but my instincts and all the circumstances of my nameless situation tell me that the end is sure and must be early. Go then and first read the narrative which Lanyon warned me he was to place in your hands; and if you care to hear more, turn to the confession of
>
> Your unworthy and unhappy friend,
>
> HENRY JEKYLL.

'There was a third enclosure?' asked Utterson.

'Here, sir,' said Poole, and gave into his hands a considerable packet sealed in several places.

The lawyer put it in his pocket. 'I would say nothing of this paper. If your master has fled or is dead, we may at least save his credit. It is now ten; I must go home and read these documents in quiet; but I shall be back before midnight, when we shall send for the police.'

They went out, locking the door of the theatre behind them; and Utterson, once more leaving the servants gathered about the fire in the hall, trudged back to his office to read the two narratives in which this mystery was now to be explained.

Dr Lanyon's Narrative

On the ninth of January, now four days ago, I received by the evening delivery a registered envelope, addressed in the hand of my colleague and old school-companion. Henry Jekyll. I was a good deal surprised by this; for we were by no means in the habit of correspondence; I had seen the man, dined with him, indeed, the night before; and I could imagine nothing in our intercourse that should justify the formality of registration. The contents increased my wonder; for this is how the letter ran:

10th December 18—

Dear Lanyon. — You are one of my oldest friends; and although we may have differed at times on scientific questions, I cannot remember, at least on my side, any break in our affection. There was never a day when, if you had said to me, 'Jekyll, my life, my honour, my reason, depend upon you,' I would not have sacrificed my fortune or my left hand to help you. Lanyon; my life, my honour, my reason, are all at your mercy; if you fail me tonight, I am lost. You might suppose, after this preface, that I am going to ask you for something dishonourable to grant. Judge for yourself.

I want you to postpone all other engagements for tonight — ay, even if you were summoned to the bedside of an emperor; to take a cab, unless your carriage should be actually at the door; and, with this letter in your hand for consultation, to drive straight to my house. Poole, my butler, has his orders; you will find him waiting your arrival with a locksmith. The door of my cabinet is then to be forced; and you are to go in alone; to open the glazed press (letter E) on the left hand, breaking the lock if it be shut; and to draw out, *with all its contents as they stand*, the fourth drawer from the top or (which is the same thing) the third from the bottom. In my extreme distress of mind, I have a morbid fear of misdirecting you; but even if I am in error, you may know the right drawer by its contents: some powders, a phial, and a paper book. This drawer I beg of you to carry back with you to Cavendish Square exactly as it stands.

That is the first part of the service: now for the second. You should be back, if you set out at once on the receipt of this, long before midnight; but I will leave you that amount of margin, not only in the fear of one of those obstacles that can neither be prevented nor foreseen, but because an hour when your servants are in bed is to be preferred for what will then remain to do. At midnight then, I have to ask you to be alone in your consulting-room, to admit with your own hand into the house a man who will present himself in my name, and to place in his hands the drawer that you will have brought with you from my cabinet. Then you will have played your part, and earned my gratitude completely. Five minutes afterwards, if you insist upon an explanation, you will have understood that these arrangements are of capital importance; and that by the neglect of one of them, fantastic as they must appear, you might have charged your conscience with my death or the shipwreck of my reason.

Confident as I am that you will not trifle with this appeal, my heart sinks and my hand trembles at the bare thought of such a possibility. Think of me at this hour, in a strange place, labouring under a blackness of distress that no fancy can exaggerate, and yet well aware that, if you will but punctually serve me, my troubles will roll away like a story that is told. Serve me, my dear Lanyon, and save

Your friend,
H. J.

P.S. — I had already sealed this up when a fresh terror struck upon my soul. It is possible that the post office may fail me, and this letter not come into your hands until tomorrow morning. In that case, dear Lanyon, do my errand when it shall be most convenient for you in the course of the day; and once more expect my messenger at midnight. It may then already be too late; and if that night passes without event, you will know that you have seen the last of Henry Jekyll.

Upon the reading of this letter, I made sure my colleague was insane; but till that was proved beyond the possibility of doubt, I felt bound to do as he requested. The less I understood of this farrago, the less I was in a position to judge of its importance; and an appeal so worded could not be set aside without a grave responsibility. I rose accordingly from table, got into a hansom, and drove straight to Jekyll's house. The butler was awaiting my arrival; he had received by the same post as mine a registered letter of instruction, and had sent at once for a locksmith and a carpenter. The tradesmen came while we were yet speaking; and we moved in a body to old Dr Denman's surgical theatre, from which (as you are doubtless aware) Jekyll's private cabinet is most conveniently entered. The door was very strong, the lock excellent; the carpenter avowed he would have great trouble, and have to do much damage, if force were to be used; and the locksmith was near despair. But this last was a handy fellow, and after two hours' work, the door stood open. The press marked E was unlocked; and I took out the drawer, had it filled up with straw and tied in a sheet, and returned with it to Cavendish Square.

Here I proceeded to examine its contents. The powders were neatly enough made up, but not with the nicety of the dispensing chemist; so that it was plain they were of Jekyll's private manufacture; and when I opened one of the wrappers, I found what seemed to me a simple crystalline salt of a white colour. The phial, to which I next turned my attention, might have been about half full of a blood-red liquor, which was highly pungent to the sense of smell, and seemed to me to contain phosphorus and some volatile ether. At the other ingredients I could make no guess. The book was an ordinary version book, and contained little but a series of dates. These covered a period of many years; but I observed that the entries ceased nearly a year ago, and quite abruptly. Here and there a brief remark was appended to a date, usually no more than a single word: 'double' occurring perhaps six times in a total of several hundred entries; and once very early in the list, and followed by several marks of exclamation, 'total failure!!!' All this, though it whetted my curiosity, told me little that was definite. Here were a phial of some tincture, a paper of some salt, and the record of a series of experiments that had led (like too many of Jekyll's investigations) to no end of practical usefulness. How could the presence of these articles in my house affect either the honour, the sanity, or the life of my flighty colleague? If his messenger could go to one place, why could he not go to another? And even granting some impediment, why was this gentleman to be received by me in secret? The more I reflected, the more convinced I grew that I was dealing with a case of cerebral disease; and though I dismissed my servants to bed, I loaded an old revolver, that I might be found in some posture of self-defence.

Twelve o'clock had scarce rung out over

London, ere the knocker sounded very gently on the door. I went myself at the summons, and found a small man crouching against the pillars of the portico.

'Are you come from Dr Jekyll?' I asked.

He told me 'yes' by a constrained gesture; and when I had bidden him enter, he did not obey me without a searching backward glance into the darkness of the square. There was a policeman not far off, advancing with his bull's-eye open; and at the sight, I thought my visitor started and made greater haste.

These particulars struck me, I confess, disagreeably; and as I followed him into the bright light of the consulting-room, I kept my hand ready on my weapon. Here, at last, I had a chance of clearly seeing him. I had never set eyes on him before, so much was certain. He was small, as I have said; I was struck besides with the shocking expression of his face, with his remarkable combination of great muscular activity and great apparent debility of constitution, and — last but not least — with the odd, subjective disturbance caused by his neighbourhood. This bore some resemblance to incipient rigor, and was accompanied by a marked sinking of the pulse. At the time, I set it down to some idiosyncratic, personal distaste, and merely wondered at the acuteness of the symptoms;

but I have since had reason to believe the cause to lie much deeper in the nature of man, and to turn on some nobler hinge than the principle of hatred.

This person (who had thus, from the first moment of his entrance, struck in me what I can only describe as a disgustful curiosity) was dressed in a fashion that would have made an ordinary person laughable; his clothes, that is to say, although they were of rich and sober fabric, were enormously too large for him in every measurement — the trousers hanging on his legs and rolled up to keep them from the ground, the waist of the coat below his haunches, and the collar sprawling wide upon his shoulders. Strange to relate, this ludicrous accoutrement was far from moving me to laughter. Rather, as there was something abnormal and misbegotten in the very essence of the creature that now faced me — something seizing, surprising and revolting — this fresh disparity seemed but to fit in with and to reinforce it; so that to my interest in the man's nature and character there was added a curiosity as to his origin, his life, his fortune and status in the world.

These observations, though they have taken so great a space to be set down in, were yet the work of a few seconds. My visitor was, indeed, on fire with sombre excitement.

'Have you got it?' he cried. 'Have you got it?' And so lively was his impatience that he even laid his hand upon my arm and sought to shake me.

I put him back, conscious at his touch of a certain icy pang along my blood. 'Come, sir,' said I. 'You forget that I have not yet the pleasure of your acquaintance. Be seated, if you please.' And I showed him an example, and sat down myself in my customary seat and with as fair an imitation of my ordinary manner to a patient as the lateness of the hour, the nature of my pre-occupations, and the horror I had of my visitor would suffer me to muster.

'I beg your pardon, Dr Lanyon,' he replied, civilly enough, 'What you say is very well founded; and my impatience has shown its heels to my politeness. I come here at the instance of your colleague, Dr Henry Jekyll, on a piece of business of some moment; and I understood . . . ' he paused and put his hand to his throat, and I could see, in spite of his collected manner, that he was wrestling against the approaches of the hysteria — 'I understood, a drawer . . . '

But here I took pity on my visitor's suspense, and some perhaps on my own growing curiosity.

'There it is, sir,' said I, pointing to the

drawer, where it lay on the floor behind a table, and still covered with the sheet.

He sprang to it, and then paused, and laid his hand upon his heart; I could hear his teeth grate with the convulsive action of his jaws; and his face was so ghastly to see that I grew alarmed both for his life and reason.

'Compose yourself,' said I.

He turned a dreadful smile to me, and, as if with the decision of despair, plucked away the sheet. At sight of the contents, he uttered one loud sob of such immense relief that I sat petrified. And the next moment, in a voice that was already fairly well under control, 'Have you a graduated glass?' he asked.

I rose from my place with something of an effort, and gave him what he asked.

He thanked me with a smiling nod, measured out a few minims of the red tincture and added one of the powders. The mixture, which was at first of a reddish hue, began, in proportion as the crystals melted, to brighten in colour, to effervesce audibly, and to throw off small fumes of vapour. Suddenly, and at the same moment, the ebullition ceased, and the compound changed to a dark purple, which faded again more slowly to a watery green. My visitor, who had watched these metamorphoses with a keen eye, smiled, set down the glass upon the table, and then turned and looked upon me with an air of scrutiny.

'And now,' said he, 'to settle what remains. Will you be wise? will you be guided? will you suffer me to take this glass in my hand, and to go forth from your house without further parley? or has the greed of curiosity too much command of you? Think before you answer, for it shall be done as you decide. As you decide, you shall be left as you were before, and neither richer nor wiser, unless the sense of service rendered to a man in mortal distress may be counted as a kind of riches of the soul. Or, if you shall so prefer to choose, a new province of knowledge and new avenues to fame and power shall be laid open to you, here, in this room, upon the instant; and your sight shall be blasted by a prodigy to stagger the unbelief of Satan.'

'Sir,' said I, affecting a coolness that I was far from truly possessing, 'you speak enigmas, and you will perhaps not wonder that I hear you with no very strong impression of belief. But I have gone too far in the way of inexplicable services to pause before I see the end.'

'It is well,' replied my visitor. 'Lanyon, you remember your vows: what follows is under the seal of our profession. And now, you who have so long been bound to the most narrow and material views, you who have denied the virtue of transcendental medicine, you who have derided your superiors — behold!'

He put the glass to his lips, and drank at one gulp. A cry followed; he reeled, staggered, clutched at the table and held on, staring with injected eyes, gasping with open mouth; and as I looked, there came, I thought, a change — he seemed to swell — his face became suddenly black, and the features seemed to melt and alter — and the next moment I had sprung to my feet and leaped back against the wall, my arm raised to shield me from that prodigy, my mind submerged in terror.

'O God!' I screamed, and 'O God!' again and again; for there before my eyes — pale and shaken, and half fainting, and groping before him with his hands, like a man restored from death — there stood Henry Jekyll!

What he told me in the next hour I cannot bring my mind to set on paper. I saw what I saw, I heard what I heard, and my soul sickened at it; and yet, now when that sight has faded from my eyes I ask myself if I believe it, and I cannot answer. My life is shaken to its roots; sleep has left me; the deadliest terror sits by me at all hours of the day and night; I feel that my days are numbered, and that I must die; and yet I shall die incredulous. As for the moral turpitude that man unveiled to me, even with tears of penitence, I cannot, even in memory, dwell on it without a start of horror. I will say but one thing, Utterson, and that (if you can bring your mind to credit it) will be more than enough. The creature who crept into my house that night was, on Jekyll's own confession, known by the name of Hyde and hunted for in every corner of the land as the murderer of Carew.

HASTIE LANYON.

Henry Jekyll's Full Statement of the Case

I was born in the year 18— to a large fortune, endowed besides with excellent parts, inclined by nature to industry, fond of the respect of the wise and good among my fellow-men, and thus, as might have been supposed, with every guarantee of an honourable and distinguished future. And indeed, the worst of my faults was a certain impatient gaiety of disposition, such as has made the happiness of many, but such as I found it hard to reconcile with my imperious desire to carry my head high, and wear a more than commonly grave countenance before the public. Hence it came about that I concealed my pleasures; and that when I reached years of reflection, and began to look round me, and take stock of my progress and position in the world, I stood already committed to a profound duplicity of life. Many a man would have even blazoned such irregularities as I was guilty of; but from the high views that I had set before me, I regarded and hid them with an almost morbid sense of shame. It was thus rather the exacting nature of my aspirations, than any particular degradation in my faults, that made me what I was, and, with even a deeper trench than in the majority of men, severed in me those provinces of good and ill which divide and compound man's dual nature. In this case, I was driven to reflect deeply and inveterately on that hard law of life which lies at the root of religion, and is one of the most plentiful springs of distress. Though so profound a double-dealer, I was in no sense a hypocrite; both sides of me were in dead earnest; I was no more myself when I laid aside restraint and plunged in shame, than when I laboured, in the eye of day, at the furtherance of knowledge or the relief of sorrow and suffering. And it chanced that the direction of my scientific studies, which led wholly towards the mystic and the transcendental, reacted and shed a strong light on this consciousness of the perennial war among my members. With every day, and from both sides of my intelligence, the moral and the intellectual, I thus drew steadily nearer to that truth by whose partial discovery I have been doomed to such a dreadful shipwreck: that man is not truly one, but truly two. I say two, because the state of my own knowledge does not pass beyond that point. Others will follow, others will outstrip me on the same lines; and I hazard the guess that man will be ultimately known for a mere polity of multifarious, incongruous, and independent denizens. I, for my part, from the nature of my life, advanced infallibly in one direction, and in one direction only. It was on the moral side, and in my own person, that I learned to recognise the thorough and primitive duality of man; I saw that, of the two natures that contended in the field of my consciousness, even if I could rightly be said to be either, it was only because I was radically both; and from an early date, even before the course of my scientific discoveries had begun to suggest the most naked possibility of such a miracle, I had learned to dwell with pleasure, as a beloved daydream, on the thought of the separation of these elements. If each, I told myself, could but be housed in separate identities, life would be relieved of all that was unbearable; the unjust might go his way, delivered from the aspirations and remorse of his more upright twin; and the just could walk steadfastly and securely on his upward path, doing the good things in which he found his pleasure, and no longer exposed to disgrace and penitence by the hands of this extraneous evil. It was the curse of mankind that these incongruous faggots were thus bound together — that in the agonised womb of consciousness these polar twins should be continuously struggling. How, then, were they dissociated?

I was so far in my reflections, when, as I have said, a side light began to shine upon the subject from the laboratory table. I began to perceive more deeply than it has ever yet been stated, the trembling immateriality, the mist-like transience, of this seemingly so solid body in which we walk attired. Certain agents I found to have the power to shake and to pluck back that fleshly vestment, even as a wind might toss the curtains of a pavilion. For two good reasons, I will not enter deeply into this scientific branch of my confession. First, because I have been made to learn that the doom and burthen of our life is bound for ever on man's shoulders; and when the attempt is made to cast it off, it but returns upon us with more unfamiliar and more awful pressure. Second, because, as my narrative will make, alas I too evident, my discoveries were incomplete. Enough, then, that I not only recognised my natural body for the mere aura and effulgence of certain of the powers that made up my spirit, but managed to compound a drug by which these powers should be dethroned from their supremacy, and a second form and countenance substituted, none the less natural to me because they were the expression, and bore the stamp, of lower elements in my soul.

I hesitated long before I put this theory to the test of practice. I knew well that I risked death; for any drug that so potently controlled and shook the very fortress of identity, might by the least scruple of an overdose or at the least inopportunity in the moment of exhibition, utterly blot out that immaterial tabernacle which I looked to it to change. But the temptation of a discovery so singular and profound at last overcame the suggestions of alarm. I had long since prepared my tincture; I purchased at once, from a firm of wholesale chemists, a large quantity of a particular salt, which I knew, from my experiments, to be the last ingredient required; and, late one accursed night, I compounded the elements, watched them boil and smoke together in the glass, and when the ebullition had subsided, with a strong glow of courage, drank off the potion.

The most racking pangs succeeded: a grinding in the bones, deadly nausea, and a horror of the spirit that cannot be exceeded at the hour of birth or death. Then these agonies began swiftly to subside, and I came to myself as if out of a great sickness. There was something strange in my sensations, something indescribably new, and, from its very novelty, incredibly sweet. I felt younger, lighter, happier in body; within I was conscious of a heady recklessness, a current of disordered sensual images running like a mill race in my fancy, a solution of the bonds of obligation, an unknown but not an innocent freedom of the soul. I knew myself, at the first breath of this new life, to be more wicked, tenfold more wicked, sold a slave to my original evil; and the thought, in that moment, braced and delighted me like wine. I stretched out my hands, exulting in the freshness of these sensations; and in the act, I was suddenly aware that I had lost in stature.

There was no mirror, at that date, in my room; that which stands beside me as I write was brought there later on, and for the very purpose of those transformations. The night, however, was far gone into the morning — the morning, black as it was, was nearly ripe for the conception of the day — the inmates of my house were locked in the most rigorous hours of slumber; and I determined, flushed as I was with hope and triumph, to venture in my new shape as far as to my bedroom. I crossed the yard, wherein the constellations looked down upon me, I could have thought, with wonder, the first creature of that sort that their unsleeping vigilance had yet disclosed to them; I stole through the corridors, a stranger in my own house; and coming to my room, I saw for the first time the appearance of Edward Hyde.

I must here speak by theory alone, saying not that which I know, but that which I suppose to be most probable. The evil side of my nature, to which I had now transferred the stamping efficacy, was less robust and less developed than the good which I had just deposed. Again, in the course of my life, which had been, after all, nine-tenths a life of effort, virtue and control, it had been much less exercised and much less exhausted. And hence, as I think, it came about that Edward Hyde was so much smaller, slighter, and younger than Henry Jekyll. Even as good shone upon the countenance of the one, evil was written broadly and plainly on the face of the other. Evil besides (which I must still believe to be the lethal side of man) had left on that body an imprint of deformity and decay. And yet when I looked upon that ugly idol in the glass, I was conscious of no repugnance, rather of a leap of welcome. This, too, was myself. It seemed natural and human. In my eyes it bore a livelier image of the spirit, it seemed more express and single, than the imperfect and divided countenance I had been hitherto accustomed to call mine. And in so far I was doubtless right. I have observed that when I wore the semblance of Edward Hyde, none could come near to me at first without a visible misgiving of the flesh. This, as I take it, was because all human beings, as we meet them, are commingled out of good and evil: and Edward Hyde, alone, in the ranks of mankind, was pure evil.

I lingered but a moment at the mirror: the second and conclusive experiment had yet to be attempted; it yet remained to be seen if I had lost my identity beyond redemption and must flee before daylight from a house that was no longer mine: and hurrying back to my cabinet, I once more prepared and drank the cup, once more suffered the pangs of dissolution, and came to myself once more with the character, the stature, and the face of Henry Jekyll.

That night I had come to the fatal cross-roads. Had I approached my discovery in a more noble spirit, had I risked the experiment while under the empire of generous or pious aspirations, all must have been otherwise, and from these agonies of death and birth I had come forth an angel instead of a fiend. The drug had no discriminating action; it was neither diabolical nor divine; it but shook the doors of the prison-house of my disposition; and, like the captives of Philippi, that which stood within ran forth. At that time my virtue slumbered; my evil, kept awake by ambition, was alert and swift to seize the occasion; and the thing that was projected was Edward Hyde. Hence, although I had now two characters as well as two appearances, one was wholly evil, and the other was still the old Henry Jekyll, that incongruous compound of whose reformation and improvement I had already learned to despair. The movement was thus wholly toward the worse.

Even at that time, I had not yet conquered my aversion to the dryness of a life of study. I would still be merrily disposed at times; and as my pleasures were (to say the least) undignified, and I was not only well known and highly considered, but growing towards the elderly man, this incoherency of my life was daily growing more unwelcome. It was on this side that my new power tempted me until I fell in slavery. I had but to drink the cup, to doff at once the body of the noted professor, and to assume, like a thick cloak, that of Edward Hyde. I smiled at the notion; it seemed to me at the time to be humorous; and I made my preparations with the most studious care. I took and furnished that house in Soho to which Hyde was tracked by the police; and engaged as housekeeper a creature whom I well knew to be silent and unscrupulous. On the other side, I announced to my servants that a Mr Hyde (whom I described) was to have full liberty and power about my house in the square; and, to parry mishaps, I even called and made myself a familiar object in my second character. I next drew up that will to which you so much objected; so that if anything befell me in the person of Dr Jekyll, I could enter on that of Edward Hyde without pecuniary loss. And thus fortified, as I supposed, on every side I began to profit by the strange immunities of my position.

Men have before hired bravos to transact their crimes, while their own person and reputation sat under shelter. I was the first that ever did so for his pleasures. I was the first that could thus plod in the public eye with a load of genial respectability, and in a moment, like a schoolboy, strip off these lendings and spring headlong into the sea of liberty. But for me, in my impenetrable mantle, the safety was complete. Think of it — I did not even exist! Let me but escape into my laboratory door, give me but a second or two to mix and swallow the draught that I had always standing ready, and, whatever he had done, Edward Hyde would pass away like the stain of breath upon a mirror; and there in his stead, quietly at home, trimming the midnight lamp in his study, a man who could afford to laugh at suspicion, would be Henry Jekyll.

The pleasures which I made haste to seek in my disguise were, as I have said, undignified; I would scarce use a harder term. But in the hands of Edward Hyde they soon began to turn towards the monstrous. When I would come back from these excursions, I was often plunged into a kind of wonder at my vicarious depravity. This familiar that I called out of my own soul, and sent forth alone to do his good pleasure, was a being inherently malign and villainous; his every act and thought centred on self; drinking pleasure with bestial avidity from any degree of torture to another; relentless like a man of stone. Henry Jekyll stood at times aghast before the acts of Edward Hyde; but the situation was apart from ordinary laws, and insidiously relaxed the grasp of conscience. It was Hyde, after all, and Hyde alone, that was guilty. Jekyll was no worse; he woke again to his good qualities seemingly unimpaired; he would even make haste, where it was possible, to undo the evil done by Hyde. And thus his conscience slumbered.

Into the details of the infamy at which I thus connived (for even now I can scarce grant that I committed it) I have no design of entering. I mean but to point out the warnings and the successive steps with which my chastisement approached. I met with one accident which, as it brought on no consequence, I shall no more than mention. An act of cruelty to a child aroused against me the anger of a passer-by, whom I recognised the other day in the person of your kinsman; the doctor and the child's family joined him; there were moments when I feared for my life; and at last, in order to pacify their too just resentment, Edward Hyde had to bring them to the door, and pay them in a cheque drawn in the name of Henry Jekyll. But this danger was easily eliminated from the future by opening an account at another bank in the name of Edward Hyde himself; and when, by sloping my own hand backwards, I had supplied my double with a signature, I thought I sat beyond the reach of fate.

Some two months before the murder of Sir Danvers, I had been out for one of my adventures, had returned at a late hour, and woke the next day in bed with somewhat odd sensations. It was in vain I looked about me; in vain I saw the decent furniture and tall proportions of my room in the square; in vain that I recognised the pattern of the bed curtains and the design of the mahogany frame; something still kept insisting that I was not where I was, that I had not wakened where I seemed to be, but in the little room in Soho where I was accustomed to sleep in the body of Edward Hyde. I smiled to myself, and, in my psychological way, began lazily to inquire into the elements of this illusion, occasionally, even as I did so, dropping back into a comfortable morning doze. I was still so engaged when, in one of my more wakeful moments, my eye fell upon my hand. Now, the hand of Henry Jekyll (as you have often remarked) was professional in shape and size; it was large, firm, white and comely. But the hand which I now saw, clearly enough in the yellow light of a mid-London morning, lying half shut on the bed-clothes, was lean, corded, knuckly, of a dusky pallor, and thickly shaded with a swart growth of hair. It was the hand of Edward Hyde.

I must have stared upon it for near half a minute, sunk as I was in the mere stupidity of wonder, before terror woke up in my breast as sudden and startling as the crash of cymbals; and bounding from my bed, I rushed to the mirror. At the sight that met my eyes, my blood was changed into something exquisitely thin and icy. Yes, I had gone to bed Henry Jekyll, I had awakened Edward Hyde. How was this to be explained? I asked myself; and then, with another bound of terror — how was it to be remedied? It was well on in the morning; the servants were up; all my drugs were in the cabinet — a long journey, down two pair of stairs, through the back passage, across the open court and through the anatomical theatre, from where I was then standing horror-struck. It might indeed be possible to cover my face; but of what use was that, when I was unable to conceal the alteration in my stature? And then, with an overpowering sweetness of relief, it came back upon my mind that the servants were already used to the coming and going of my second self. I had soon dressed, as well as I was able, in clothes of my own size; had soon passed through the house, where Bradshaw stared and drew back at seeing Mr Hyde at such an hour and in such a strange array; and ten minutes later, Dr Jekyll had returned to his own shape, and was sitting down, with a darkened brow, to make a feint of breakfasting.

Small indeed was my appetite. This inexplicable incident, this reversal of my previous experience, seemed, like the Babylonian finger on the wall, to be spelling out the letters of my judgment; and I began to reflect more seriously than ever before on the issues and possibilities of my double existence. That part of me which I had the power of projecting had lately been much exercised and nourished; it had seemed to me of late as though the body of Edward Hyde had grown in stature, as though (when I wore that form) I were conscious of a more generous tide of blood; and I began to spy a danger that, if this were much prolonged, the balance of my nature might be permanently overthrown, the power of voluntary change be forfeited, and the character of Edward Hyde become irrevocably mine. The power of the drug had not been always equally displayed. Once, very early in my career, it had totally failed me; since then I had been obliged on more than one occasion to double, and once, with infinite risk of death, to treble the amount; and these rare uncertainties had cast hitherto the sole shadow on my contentment. Now, however, and in the light of that morning's accident, I was led to remark that whereas, in the beginning, the difficulty had been to throw off the body of Jekyll, it had of late gradually but decidedly transferred itself to the other side. All things therefore seemed to point to this: that I was slowly losing hold of my original and better self, and becoming slowly incorporated with my second and worse.

Between these two I now felt I had to choose. My two natures had memory in common, but all other faculties were most unequally shared between them. Jekyll (who was composite), now with the most sensitive apprehensions, now with a greedy gusto, projected and shared in the pleasures and adventures of Hyde; but Hyde was indifferent to Jekyll, or but remembered him as the mountain bandit remembers the cavern in which he conceals himself from pursuit. Jekyll had more than a father's interest; Hyde had more than a son's indifference. To cast in my lot with Jekyll was to die to those appetites which I had long secretly indulged and had of late begun to pamper. To cast it in with Hyde was to die to a thousand interests and aspirations, and to become, at a blow and for ever, despised and friendless. The bargain might appear unequal; but there was still another consideration in the scales; for while Jekyll would suffer smartingly in the fires of abstinence, Hyde would be not even conscious of all that he had lost. Strange as my circumstances were, the terms of this debate are as old and common-place as man; much the same inducements and alarms cast the die for any tempted and trembling sinner; and it fell out with me, as it falls with so vast a majority of my fellows, that I chose the better part, and was found wanting in the strength to keep to it.

Yes, I preferred the elderly and discontented doctor, surrounded by friends, and cherishing honest hopes; and bade a resolute farewell to the liberty, the comparative youth, the light step, leaping pulses and secret pleasures, that I had enjoyed in the disguise of Hyde. I made this choice perhaps with some unconscious reservation, for I neither gave up the house in Soho, nor destroyed the clothes of Edward Hyde, which still lay ready in my cabinet. For two months, however, I was true to my determination; for two months I led a life of such severity as I had never before attained to, and enjoyed the compensations of an approving conscience. But time began at last to obliterate the freshness of my alarm; the praises of conscience began to grow into a thing of course; I began to be tortured with throes and longings, as of Hyde struggling after freedom; and at last, in an hour of moral weakness, I once again compounded and swallowed the transforming draught.

I do not suppose that when a drunkard reasons with himself upon his vice, he is once out of five hundred times affected by the dangers that he runs through his brutish physical insensibility; neither had I, long as I had considered my position, made enough allowance for the complete moral insensibility and insensate readiness to evil which were the leading characters of Edward Hyde. Yet it was by these that I was punished. My devil had been long caged, he came out roaring. I was conscious, even when I took the draught, of a more unbridled, a more furious propensity to ill. It must have been this, I suppose, that stirred in my soul that tempest of impatience with which I listened to the civilities of my unhappy victim; I declare at least, before God, no man morally sane could have been guilty of that crime upon so pitiful a provocation; and that I struck in no more reasonable spirit than that in which a sick child may break a plaything. But I had voluntarily stripped myself of all those balancing instincts by which even the worst of us continues to walk with some degree of steadiness among temptations; and in my case, to be tempted, however slightly, was to fall.

Instantly the spirit of hell awoke in me and raged. With a transport of glee, I mauled the unresisting body, tasting delight from every blow; and it was not till weariness had begun to succeed that I was suddenly, in the top fit of my delirium, struck through the heart by a cold thrill of terror. A mist dispersed; I saw my life to be forfeit; and fled from the scene of these excesses, at once glorying and trembling, my lust of evil gratified and stimulated, my love of life screwed to the topmost peg. I ran to the house in Soho, and (to make assurance doubly sure) destroyed my papers; thence I set out through the lamplit streets, in the same divided ecstasy of mind, gloating on my crime, light-headedly devising others in the future, and yet still hastening and still harkening in my wake for the steps of the avenger. Hyde had a song upon his lips as he compounded the draught, and as he drank it pledged the dead man. The pangs of transformation had not done tearing him, before Henry Jekyll, with streaming tears of gratitude and remorse, had fallen upon his knees and lifted his clasped hands to God. The veil of self-indulgence was rent from head to foot, I saw my life as a whole: I followed it up from the days of childhood, when I had walked with my father's hand, and through the self-denying toils of my professional life, to arrive again and again, with the same sense of unreality, at the damned horrors of the evening. I could have screamed aloud; I sought with tears and prayers to smother down the crowd of hideous images and sounds with which my memory swarmed against me; and still, between the petitions, the ugly face of my iniquity stared into my soul. As the acuteness of this remorse began to die away, it was succeeded by a sense of joy. The problem of my conduct was solved. Hyde was thenceforth impossible; whether I would or not, I was now confined to the better part of my existence; and, oh, how I rejoiced to think it! with what willing humility I embraced anew the restrictions of natural life! with what sincere renunciation I locked the door by which I had so often gone and come, and ground the key under my heel!

The next day came the news that the murder had been over-looked, that the guilt of Hyde was patent to the world, and that the victim was a man high in public estimation. It was not only a crime, it had been a tragic folly. I think I was glad to know it; I think I was glad to have my better impulses thus buttressed and guarded by the terrors of the scaffold. Jekyll was now my city of refuge; let but Hyde peep out an instant, and the hands of all men would be raised to take and slay him.

I resolved in my future conduct to redeem the past; and I can say with honesty that my resolve was fruitful of some good. You know yourself how earnestly in the last months of last year I laboured to relieve suffering; you know that much was done for others, and that the days passed quietly, almost happily for myself. Nor can I truly say that I wearied of this beneficent and innocent life; I think instead that I daily enjoyed it more completely; but I was still cursed with my duality of purpose; and as the first edge of my penitence wore off, the lower side of me, so long indulged, so recently chained down, began to growl for licence. Not that I dreamed of resuscitating Hyde; the bare idea of that would startle me to frenzy: no, it was in my own person that I was once more tempted to trifle with my conscience; and it was as an ordinary secret sinner that I at last fell before the assaults of temptation.

There comes an end to all things; the most capacious measure is filled at last; and this brief condescension to my evil finally destroyed the balance of my soul. And yet I was not alarmed; the fall seemed natural, like a return to the old days before I had made my discovery. It was a fine, clear January day, wet under foot where the frost had melted, but cloudless overhead; and the Regent's Park was full of winter chirrupings and sweet with spring odours. I sat in the sun on a bench; the animal within me licking the chops of memory; the spiritual side a little drowsed, promising subsequent penitence, but not yet moved to begin. After all, I reflected, I was like my neighbours; and then I smiled, comparing myself with other men, comparing my active goodwill with the lazy cruelty of their neglect. And at the very moment of that vainglorious thought, a qualm came over me, a horrid nausea and the most deadly shuddering. These passed away, and left me faint; and then as in its turn the faintness subsided, I began to be aware of a change in the temper of my thoughts, a greater boldness, a contempt of danger, a solution of the bonds of obligation I looked down; my clothes hung formlessly on my shrunken limbs; the hand that lay on my knee was corded and hairy. I was once more Edward Hyde. A moment before I had been safe of all men's respect, wealthy, beloved — the cloth laying for me in the dining-room at home; and now I was the common quarry of mankind, hunted, houseless, a known murderer, thrall to the gallows.

My reason wavered, but it did not fail me utterly. I have more than once observed that, in my second character, my faculties seemed sharpened to a point and my spirits more tensely elastic; thus it came about that, where Jekyll perhaps might have succumbed, Hyde rose to the importance of the moment. My drugs were in one of the presses of my cabinet: how was I to reach them? That was the problem that (crushing my temples in my hands) I set myself to solve. The laboratory door I had closed. If I sought to enter by the house, my own servants would consign me to the gallows. I saw I must employ another hand, and thought of Lanyon. How was he to be reached? how persuaded? Supposing that I escaped capture in the streets, how was I to make my way into his presence? and how should I, an unknown and displeasing visitor, prevail on the famous physician to rifle the study of his colleague, Dr Jekyll? Then I remembered that of my original character, one part remained to me: I could write my own hand; and once I had conceived that kindling spark, the way that I must follow became lighted up from end to end.

Thereupon, I arranged my clothes as best I could, and summoning a passing hansom, drove to an hotel in Portland Street, the name of which I chanced to remember. At my appearance (which was indeed comical enough, however tragic a fate these garments covered) the driver could not conceal his mirth. I gnashed my teeth upon him with a gust of devilish fury; and the smile withered from his face — happily for him — yet more happily for myself, for in another instant I had certainly dragged him from his perch. At the inn, as I entered, I looked about me with so black a countenance as made the attendants tremble; not a look did they exchange in my presence; but obsequiously took my orders, led me to a private room, and brought me wherewithal to write. Hyde in danger of his life was a creature new to me: shaken with inordinate anger, strung to the pitch of murder, lusting to inflict pain. Yet the creature was astute; mastered his fury with a great effort of the will; composed his two important letters, one to Lanyon and one to Poole, and, that he might receive actual evidence of their being posted, sent them out with directions that they should be registered.

Thenceforward, he sat all day over the fire in the private room, gnawing his nails; there he dined, sitting alone with his fears, the waiter visibly quailing before his eye; and thence, when the night was fully come, he set forth in the corner of a closed cab, and was driven to and fro about the streets of the city. He, I say — I cannot say, I. That child of Hell had nothing human; nothing lived in him but fear and hatred. And when at last, thinking the driver had begun to grow suspicious, he discharged the cab and ventured on foot, attired in his misfitting clothes, an object marked out for observation, into the midst of the nocturnal passengers, these two base passions raged within him like a tempest. He walked fast, hunted by his fears, chattering to himself, skulking through the less frequented thoroughfares, counting the minutes that still divided him from midnight. Once a woman spoke to him, offering, I think, a box of lights. He smote her in the face, and she fled.

When I came to myself at Lanyon's, the horror of my old friend perhaps affected me somewhat: I do not know; it was at least but a drop in the sea to the abhorrence with which I looked back upon these hours. A change had come over me. It was no longer the fear of the gallows, it was the horror of being Hyde that racked me. I received Lanyon's condemnation partly in a dream; it was partly in a dream that I came home to my own house and got into bed. I slept after the prostration of the day, with a stringent and profound slumber which not even the nightmares that wrung me could avail to break. I awoke in the morning shaken, weakened, but refreshed. I still hated and feared the thought of the brute that slept within me, and I had not of course forgotten the appalling dangers of the day before; but I was once more at home, in my own house and close to my drugs; and gratitude for my escape shone so strong in my soul that it almost rivalled the brightness of hope.

I was stepping leisurely across the court after breakfast, drinking the chill of the air with pleasure, when I was seized again with those indescribable sensations that heralded the change; and I had but the time to gain the shelter of my cabinet, before I was once again raging and freezing with the passions of Hyde. It took on this occasion a double dose to recall me to myself; and, alas! six hours after, as I sat looking sadly in the fire, the pangs returned, and the drug had to be re-administered. In short, from that day forth it seemed only by a great effort as of gymnastics, and only under the immediate stimulation of the drug, that I was able to wear the countenance of Jekyll. At all hours of the day and night I would be taken with the premonitory shudder; above all, if I slept, or even dozed for a moment in my chair, it was always as Hyde that I awakened. Under the strain of this continually impending doom and by the sleeplessness to which I now condemned myself, ay, even beyond what I had thought possible to man, I became, in my own person, a creature eaten up and emptied by fever, languidly weak both in body and mind, and solely occupied by one thought: the horror of my other self. But when I slept, or when the virtue of the medicine wore off, I would leap almost without transition (for the pangs of transformation grew daily less marked) into the possession of a fancy brimming with images of terror, a soul boiling with causeless hatreds, and a body that seemed not strong enough to contain the raging energies of life. The powers of Hyde seemed to have grown with the sickliness of Jekyll. And certainly the hate that now divided them was equal on each side. With Jekyll, it was a thing of vital instinct. He had now seen the full deformity of that creature that shared with him some of the phenomena of consciousness, and was co-heir with him to death: and beyond these links of community, which in themselves made the most poignant part of his distress, he thought of Hyde, for all his energy of life, as of something not only hellish but inorganic. This was the shocking thing; that the slime of the pit seemed to utter cries and voices; that the amorphous dust gesticulated and sinned; that what was dead, and had no shape, should usurp the offices of life. And this again, that that insurgent horror was knit to him closer than a wife, closer than an eye; lay caged in his flesh, where he heard it mutter and felt it struggle to be born; and at every hour of weakness, and in the confidence of slumber, prevailed against him, and deposed him out of life. The hatred of Hyde for Jekyll was of a different order. His terror of the gallows drove him continually to commit temporary suicide, and return to his subordinate station of a part instead of a person; but he loathed the necessity, he loathed the despondency into which Jekyll was now fallen, and he resented the dislike with which he was himself regarded. Hence the apelike tricks that he would play me, scrawling in my own hand blasphemies on the pages of my books, burning the letters and destroying the portrait of my father; and indeed, had it not been for his fear of death, he would long ago have ruined himself in order to involve me in the ruin. But his love of life is wonderful; I go further; I, who sicken and freeze at the mere thought of him, when I recall the abjection and passion of this attachment, and when I know how he fears my power to cut him off by suicide, I find it in my heart to pity him.

It is useless, and the time awfully fails me, to prolong this description; no one has ever suffered such torments, let that suffice; and yet even to these, habit brought — no, not alleviation — but a certain callousness of soul, a certain acquiescence of despair; and my punishment might have gone on for years, but for the last calamity which has now fallen, and which has finally severed me from my own face and nature. My provision of the salt, which had never been renewed since the date of the first experiment, began to run low. I sent out for a fresh supply, and mixed the draught; the ebullition followed, and the first change of colour, not the second; I drank it, and it was without efficiency. You will learn from Poole how I have had London ransacked; it was in vain; and I am now persuaded that my first supply was impure, and that it was that unknown impurity which lent efficacy to the draught.

About a week has passed, and I am now finishing this statement under the influence of the last of the old powders. This, then, is the last time, short of a miracle, that Henry Jekyll can think his own thoughts or see his own face (now how sadly altered!) in the glass. Nor must I delay too long to bring my writing to an end; for if my narrative has hitherto escaped destruction, it has been by a combination of great prudence and great good luck. Should the throes of change take me in the act of writing it, Hyde will tear it in pieces; but if some time shall have elapsed after I have laid it by, his wonderful selfishness and circumscription to the moment will probably save it once again from the action of his apelike spite. And indeed the doom that is closing on us both has already changed and crushed him. Half an hour from now, when I shall again and for ever reindue that hated personality, I know how I shall sit shuddering and weeping in my chair, or continue, with the most strained and fear-struck ecstasy of listening, to pace up and down this room (my last earthly refuge) and give ear to every sound of menace. Will Hyde die upon the scaffold? or will he find the courage to release himself at the last moment? God knows; I am careless; this is my true hour of death, and what is to follow concerns another than myself. Here, then, as I lay down the pen, and proceed to seal up my confession, I bring the life of that unhappy Henry Jekyll to an end.

'OH, WHISTLE, AND I'LL COME TO YOU, MY LAD'

M. R. James

'I suppose you will be getting away pretty soon, now Full Term is over, Professor,' said a person not in the story to the Professor of Ontography, soon after they had sat down next to each other at a feast in the hospitable hall of St James's College.

The Professor was young, neat, and precise in speech.

'Yes,' he said; 'my friends have been making me take up golf this term, and I mean to go to the East Coast — in point of fact to Burnstow — (I dare say you know it) for a week or ten days, to improve my game. I hope to get off tomorrow.'

'Oh, Parkins,' said his neighbour on the other side, 'if you are going to Burnstow, I wish you would look at the site of the Templars' preceptory, and let me know if you think it would be any good to have a dig there in the summer.'

It was, as you might suppose, a person of antiquarian pursuits who said this, but, since he merely appears in this prologue, there is no need to give his entitlements.

'Certainly,' said Parkins, the Professor: 'if

you will describe to me whereabouts the site is, I will do my best to give you an idea of the lie of the land when I get back; or I could write to you about it, if you would tell me where you are likely to be.'

'Don't trouble to do that, thanks. It's only that I'm thinking of taking my family in that direction in the Long, and it occurred to me that, as very few of the English preceptories have ever been properly planned, I might have an opportunity of doing something useful on off-days.'

The Professor rather sniffed at the idea that planning out a preceptory could be described as useful. His neighbour continued:

'The site — I doubt if there is anything showing above ground — must be down quite close to the beach now. The sea has encroached tremendously, as you know, all along that bit of coast. I should think, from the map, that it must be about three-quarters of a mile from the Globe Inn, at the north end of the town. Where are you going to stay?'

'Well, *at* the Globe Inn, as a matter of fact,' said Parkins; 'I have engaged a room there. I couldn't get in anywhere else; most of the lodging-houses are shut up in winter, it seems; and, as it is, they tell me that the only room of any size I can have is really a double-bedded one, and that they haven't a corner in which to store the other bed, and so on. But I must have a fairly large room, for I am taking some books down, and mean to do a bit of work; and though I don't quite fancy having an empty bed — not to speak of two — in what I may call for the time being my study, I suppose I can manage to rough it for the short time I shall be there.'

'Do you call having an extra bed in your room roughing it, Parkins?' said a bluff person opposite. 'Look here, I shall come down and occupy it for a bit; it'll be company for you.'

The Professor quivered, but managed to laugh in a courteous manner.

'By all means, Rogers; there's nothing I should like better. But I'm afraid you would find it rather dull; you don't play golf, do you?'

'No, thank Heaven!' said rude Mr Rogers.

'Well, you see, when I'm not writing I shall most likely be out on the links, and that, as I say, would be rather dull for you, I'm afraid.'

'Oh, I don't know! There's certain to be somebody I know in the place; but, of course, if you don't want me, speak the word, Parkins; I shan't be offended. Truth, as you always tell us, is never offensive.'

Parkins was, indeed, scrupulously polite

and strictly truthful. It is to be feared that Mr Rogers sometimes practised upon his knowledge of these characteristics. In Parkins's breast there was a conflict now raging, which for a moment or two did not allow him to answer. That interval being over, he said:

'Well, if you want the exact truth, Rogers, I was considering whether the room I speak of would really be large enough to accommodate us both comfortably; and also whether (mind, I shouldn't have said this if you hadn't pressed me) you would not constitute something in the nature of a hindrance to my work.'

Rogers laughed loudly.

'Well done, Parkins!' he said. 'It's all right. I promise not to interrupt your work; don't you disturb yourself about that. No, I won't come if you don't want me; but I thought I should do so nicely to keep the ghosts off.' Here he might have been seen to wink and to nudge his next neighbour. Parkins might also have been seen to become pink. 'I beg pardon, Parkins,' Rogers continued; 'I oughtn't to have said that. I forgot you didn't like levity on these topics.'

'Well,' Parkins said, 'as you have mentioned the matter, I freely own that I do *not* like careless talk about what you call ghosts. A man in my position,' he went on, raising his voice a little, 'cannot, I find, be too careful about appearing to sanction the current beliefs on such subjects. As you know, Rogers, or as you ought to know; for I think I have never concealed my views — '

'No, you certainly have not, old man,' put in Rogers *sotto voce*.

' — I hold that any semblance, any appearance of concession to the view that such things might exist is equivalent to a renunciation of all that I hold most sacred. But I'm afraid I have not succeeded in securing your attention.'

'Your *undivided* attention, was what Dr Blimber actually *said*,' Rogers interrupted, with every appearance of an earnest desire for accuracy. 'But I beg your pardon, Parkins: I'm stopping you.'

'No, not at all,' said Parkins. 'I don't remember Blimber; perhaps he was before my time. But I needn't go on. I'm sure you know what I mean.'

'Yes, yes,' said Rogers, rather hastily — 'Just so. We'll go into it fully at Burnstow, or somewhere.'

In repeating the above dialogue I have tried to give the impression which it made on me, that Parkins was something of an old woman — rather henlike, perhaps, in his little ways; totally destitute, alas! of the sense of humour, but at the same time dauntless and sincere in his convictions, and a man deserving of the greatest respect. Whether or not the reader has gathered so much, that was the character which Parkins had.

* * *

On the following day Parkins did, as he had hoped, succeed in getting away from his college, and in arriving at Burnstow. He was made welcome at the Globe Inn, was safely installed in the large double-bedded room of which we have heard, and was able before retiring to rest to arrange his materials for work in apple-pie order upon a commodious table which occupied the outer end of the room, and was surrounded on three sides by windows looking out seaward; that is to say, the central window looked straight out to sea, and those on the left and right commanded prospects along the shore to the north and south respectively. On the south you saw the village of Burnstow. On the north no houses were to be seen, but only the beach and the low cliff backing it. Immediately in front was a strip — not considerable — of rough grass, dotted with old anchors, capstans, and so forth; then a broad path; then the beach. Whatever may have been the original distance between the Globe Inn and the sea, not more than sixty yards now separated them.

The rest of the population of the inn was, of course, a golfing one, and included few elements that call for a special description. The most conspicuous figure was, perhaps, that of an *ancien militaire*, secretary of a London club, and possessed of a voice of incredible strength, and of views of a pronouncedly Protestant type. These were apt to find utterance after his attendance upon the ministrations of the Vicar, an estimable man with inclinations towards a picturesque ritual, which he gallantly kept down as far as he could out of deference to East Anglian tradition.

Professor Parkins, one of whose principal characteristics was pluck, spent the greater part of the day following his arrival at Burnstow in what he had called improving his game, in company with this Colonel Wilson: and during the afternoon — whether the process of improvement were to blame or not, I am not sure — the Colonel's demeanour assumed a colouring so lurid that even Parkins jibbed at the thought of walking home with him from the links. He determined, after a short and furtive look at that bristling moustache and those incarnadined features, that it would be wiser to allow the influences of tea and tobacco to do what they could with the Colonel before the dinner-hour should render a meeting inevitable.

'I might walk home tonight along the beach,' he reflected — 'yes, and take a look — there will be light enough for that — at the ruins of which Disney was talking. I don't exactly know where they are, by the way; but I expect I can hardly help stumbling on them.'

This he accomplished, I may say, in the most literal sense, for in picking his way from the links to the shingle beach his foot caught, partly in a gorse-root and partly in a biggish stone, and over he went. When he got up and surveyed his surroundings, he found himself in a patch of somewhat broken ground covered with small depressions and mounds. These latter, when he came to examine them, proved to be simply masses of flints embedded in mortar and grown over with turf. He must, he quite rightly concluded, be on the site of the preceptory he had promised to look at. It seemed not unlikely to reward the spade of the explorer; enough of the foundations was probably left at no great depth to throw a good deal of light on the general plan. He remembered vaguely that the Templars, to whom this site had belonged, were in the habit of building round churches, and he thought a particular series of the humps or mounds near him did appear to be arranged in something of a circular form. Few people can resist the temptation to try a little amateur research in a department quite outside their own, if only for the satisfaction of showing how successful they would have been had they only taken it up seriously. Our Professor, however, if he felt something of this mean desire, was also truly anxious to oblige Mr Disney. So he paced with care the circular area he had noticed, and wrote down its rough dimensions in his pocket-book. Then he proceeded to examine an oblong eminence which lay east of the centre of the circle, and seemed to his thinking likely to be the base of a platform or altar. At one end of it, the northern, a patch of the turf was gone — removed by some boy or other creature *ferae naturae*. It might, he thought, be as well to probe the soil here for evidences of masonry, and he took out his knife and began scraping away the earth. And now followed another little discovery: a portion of soil fell inward as he scraped, and disclosed a small cavity. He lighted one match after another to help him to see of what nature the hole was, but the wind was too strong for them all. By tapping and scratching the sides with his knife, however, he was able to make out that it must be an artificial hole in masonry. It was rectangular, and the sides, top, and bottom, if not actually plastered, were smooth and regular. Of course it was empty. No! As he withdrew the knife he heard a metallic clink, and when he introduced his hand it met with a cylindrical object lying on the floor of the hole. Naturally enough, he picked it up, and when he brought it into the light, now fast fading, he could see that it, too, was of man's making — a metal tube about four inches long, and evidently of some considerable age.

By the time Parkins had made sure that there was nothing else in this odd receptacle, it was too late and too dark for him to think of undertaking any further search. What he had done had proved so unexpectedly interesting that he determined to sacrifice a little more of the daylight on the morrow to archaeology. The object which he now had safe in his pocket was bound to be of some slight value at least, he felt sure.

Bleak and solemn was the view on which he took a last look before starting homeward. A faint yellow light in the west showed the links, on which a few figures moving towards the club-house were still visible, the squat martello tower, the lights of Aldsey village, the pale ribbon of sands intersected at intervals by black wooden groynings, the dim and murmuring sea. The wind was bitter from the north, but was at his back when he set out for the Globe. He quickly rattled and clashed through the shingle and gained the sand, upon which, but for the groynings which had to be got over every few yards, the going was both good and quiet. One last look behind, to measure the distance he had made since leaving the ruined Templars' church, showed him a prospect of company on his walk, in the shape of a rather indistinct personage, who seemed to be making great efforts to catch up with him, but made little, if any, progress. I mean that there was an appearance of running about his movements, but that the distance between him and Parkins did not seem materially to lessen. So, at least, Parkins thought, and decided that he almost certainly did not know him, and that it would be absurd to wait until he came up. For all that, company, he began to think, would really be very welcome on that lonely shore, if only you could choose your companion. In his unenlightened days he had read of meetings in such places which even now would hardly bear thinking of. He went on thinking of them, however, until he reached home, and particularly of one which catches most people's fancy at some time of their childhood. 'Now I saw in my dream that Christian had gone but a very little way when he saw a foul fiend coming over the field to meet him.' 'What should I do now,' he thought, 'if I looked back and caught sight of a black figure sharply defined against the yellow sky, and saw that it had horns and wings? I wonder whether I should stand or run for it. Luckily, the gentleman behind is not of that kind, and he seems to be about as far off now as when I saw him first. Well, at this rate, he won't get his dinner as soon as I shall; and, dear me! it's within a quarter of an hour of the time now. I must run!'

Parkins had, in fact, very little time for dressing. When he met the Colonel at dinner, Peace — or as much of her as that gentleman could manage — reigned once more in the military bosom; nor was she put to flight in the hours of bridge that followed dinner, for Parkins was a more than respectable player. When, therefore, he retired towards twelve o'clock, he felt that he had spent his evening in quite a satisfactory way, and that, even for so long as a fortnight or three weeks, life at the Globe would be supportable under similar conditions — 'especially,' thought he, 'if I go on improving my game.'

As he went along the passages he met the boots of the Globe, who stopped and said:

‘Beg your pardon, sir, but as I was abrushing your coat just now there was something fell out of the pocket. I put it on your chest of drawers, sir, in your room, sir — a piece of a pipe or somethink of that, sir. Thank you, sir. You’ll find it on your chest of drawers, sir — yes, sir. Good night, sir.’

The speech served to remind Parkins of his little discovery of that afternoon. It was with some considerable curiosity that he turned it over by the light of his candles. It was of bronze, he now saw, and was shaped very much after the manner of the modern dog-whistle; in fact it was — yes, certainly it was — actually no more nor less than a whistle. He put it to his lips, but it was quite full of a fine, caked-up sand or earth, which would not yield to knocking, but must be loosened with a knife. Tidy as ever in his habits, Parkins cleared out the earth on to a piece of paper, and took the latter to the window to empty it out. The night was clear and bright, as he saw when he had opened the casement, and he stopped for an instant to look at the sea and note a belated wanderer stationed on the shore in front of the inn. Then he shut the window, a little surprised at the late hours people kept at Burnstow, and took his whistle to the light again. Why, surely there were marks on it, and not merely marks, but letters! A very little rubbing rendered the deeply-cut inscription quite legible, but the Professor had to confess, after some earnest thought, that the meaning of it was as obscure to him as the writing on the wall to Belshazzar. There were legends both on the front and on the back of the whistle. The one read thus:

FLA FUR BIS FLE

The other:

QUIS EST ISTE QUI VENIT

'I ought to be able to make it out,' he thought; 'but I suppose I am a little rusty in my Latin. When I come to think of it, I don't believe I even know the word for a whistle. The long one does seem simple enough. It ought to mean: 'Who is this who is coming?' Well, the best way to find out is evidently to whistle for him.'

He blew tentatively and stopped suddenly, startled and yet pleased at the note he had elicited. It had a quality of infinite distance in it, and, soft as it was, he somehow felt it must be audible for miles round. It was a sound, too, that seemed to have the power (which many scents possess) of forming pictures in the brain. He saw quite clearly for a moment a vision of a wide, dark expanse at night, with a fresh wind blowing, and in the midst a lonely figure — how employed, he could not tell. Perhaps he would have seen more had not the picture been broken by the sudden surge of a gust of wind against his casement, so sudden that it made him look up, just in time to see the white glint of a seabird's wing somewhere outside the dark panes.

The sound of the whistle had so fascinated him that he could not help trying it once more, this time more boldly. The note was little, if at all, louder than before, and repetition broke the illusion — no picture followed, as he had half hoped it might. 'But what is this? Goodness! what force the wind can get up in a few minutes! What a tremendous gust! There! I knew that window-fastening was no use! Ah! I thought so — both candles out. It is enough to tear the room to pieces.'

The first thing was to get the window shut. While you might count twenty Parkins was struggling with the small casement, and felt almost as if he were pushing back a sturdy burglar, so strong was the pressure. It slackened all at once, and the window banged to and latched itself. Now to relight the candles and see what damage, if any, had been done. No, nothing seemed amiss; no glass even was broken in the casement. But the noise had evidently roused at least one member of the household: the Colonel was to be heard stumping in his stockinged feet on the floor above, and growling. Quickly as it had risen, the wind did not fall at once. On it went, moaning and rushing past the house, at times rising to a cry so desolate that, as Parkins disinterestedly said, it might have made fanciful people feel quite uncomfortable; even the unimaginative, he thought after a quarter of an hour, might be happier without it.

Whether it was the wind, or the excitement of golf, or of the researches in the preceptory that kept Parkins awake, he was not sure. Awake he remained, in any case, long enough to fancy (as I am afraid I often do myself under such conditions) that he was the victim of all manner of fatal disorders: he would lie counting the beats of his heart, convinced that it was going to stop work every moment, and would entertain grave suspicions of his lungs, brain, liver, etc. — suspicions which he was sure would be dispelled by the return of daylight, but which until then refused to be put aside. He found a little vicarious comfort in the idea that someone else was in the same boat. A near neighbour (in the darkness it was not easy to tell his direction) was tossing and rustling in his bed, too.

The next stage was that Parkins shut his eyes and determined to give sleep every chance. Here again over-excitement asserted itself in another form — that of making pictures. *Experto crede*, pictures do come to the closed eyes of one trying to sleep, and are often so little to his taste that he must open his eyes and disperse them.

Parkins's experience on this occasion was a very distressing one. He found that the picture which presented itself to him was continuous. When he opened his eyes, of course, it went; but when he shut them once more it framed itself afresh, and acted itself out again, neither quicker nor slower than before. What he saw was this:

A long stretch of shore — shingle edged by sand, and intersected at short intervals with black groynes running down to the water — a scene, in fact, so like that of his afternoon's walk that, in the absence of any landmark, it could not be distinguished therefrom. The light was obscure, conveying an impression of gathering storm, late winter evening, and slight cold rain. On this bleak stage at first no actor was visible. Then, in the distance, a bobbing black object appeared; a moment more, and it was a man running, jumping, clambering over the groynes, and every few seconds looking eagerly back. The nearer he came the more obvious it was that he was not only anxious, but even terribly frightened, though his face was not to be distinguished. He was, moreover, almost at the end of his strength. On he came; each successive obstacle seemed to cause him more difficulty than the last. 'Will he get over this next one?' thought Parkins; 'it seems a little higher than the others.' Yes; half climbing, half throwing himself, he did get over, and fell all in a heap on the other side (the side nearest to the spectator). There, as if really unable to get up again, he remained crouching under the groyne, looking up in an attitude of painful anxiety.

So far no cause whatever for the fear of the runner had been shown; but now there began to be seen, far up the shore, a little flicker of something light-coloured moving to and fro with great swiftness and irregularity. Rapidly growing larger, it, too, declared itself as a figure in pale, fluttering draperies, ill-defined. There was something about its motion which made Parkins very unwilling to see it at close quarters. It would stop, raise arms, bow itself towards the sand, then run stooping across the beach to the water-edge and back again; and then, rising upright, once more continue its course forward at a speed that was startling and terrifying. The moment came when the pursuer was hovering about from left to right only a few yards beyond the groyne where the runner lay in hiding. After two or three ineffectual castings hither and thither it came to a stop, stood upright, with arms raised high, and then darted straight forward towards the groyne.

It was at this point that Parkins always failed in his resolution to keep his eyes shut. With many misgivings as to incipient failure of eyesight, overworked brain, excessive smoking, and so on, he finally resigned himself to light his candle, get out a book, and pass the night waking, rather than be tormented by this persistent panorama, which he saw clearly enough could only be a morbid reflection of his walk and his thoughts on that very day.

The scraping of match on box and the glare of light must have startled some creatures of the night — rats or what not — which he heard scurry across the floor from the side of his bed with much rustling. Dear, dear! the match is out! Fool that it is! But the second one burnt better, and a candle and book were duly procured, over which Parkins pored till sleep of a wholesome kind came upon him, and that in no long space.

For about the first time in his orderly and prudent life he forgot to blow out the candle, and when he was called next morning at eight there was still a flicker in the socket and a sad mess of guttered grease on the top of the little table.

After breakfast he was in his room, putting the finishing touches to his golfing costume — fortune had again allotted the Colonel to him for a partner — when one of the maids came in.

'Oh, if you please,' she said, 'would you like any extra blankets on your bed, sir?'

'Ah! thank you,' said Parkins. 'Yes, I think I should like one. It seems likely to turn rather colder.'

In a very short time the maid was back with the blanket.

'Which bed should I put it on, sir?' she asked.

'What? Why, that one — the one I slept in last night,' he said, pointing to it.

'Oh yes! I beg your pardon, sir, but you seemed to have tried both of 'em; leastways, we had to make 'em both up this morning.'

'Really? How very absurd!' said Parkins. 'I certainly never touched the other, except to lay some things on it. Did it actually seem to have been slept in?'

'Oh yes, sir!' said the maid. 'Why, all the

things was crumpled and throwed about all ways, if you'll excuse me, sir — quite as if anyone 'adn't passed but a very poor night, sir.'

'Dear me,' said Parkins. 'Well, I may have disordered it more than I thought when I unpacked my things. I'm very sorry to have given you the extra trouble, I'm sure. I expect a friend of mine soon, by the way — a gentleman from Cambridge — to come and occupy it for a night or two. That will be all right, I suppose, won't it?'

'Oh yes, to be sure, sir. Thank you, sir. It's no trouble, I'm sure,' said the maid, and departed to giggle with her colleagues.

Parkins set forth, with a stern determination to improve his game.

I am glad to be able to report that he succeeded so far in this enterprise that the Colonel, who had been rather repining at the prospect of a second day's play in his company, became quite chatty as the morning advanced; and his voice boomed out over the flats, as certain also of our own minor poets have said, 'like some great bourdon in a minster tower'.

'Extraordinary wind, that, we had last night,' he said. 'In my old home we should have said someone had been whistling for it.'

'Should you, indeed!' said Perkins. 'Is there

a superstition of that kind still current in your part of the country?'

'I don't know about superstition,' said the Colonel. 'They believe in it all over Denmark and Norway, as well as on the Yorkshire coast; and my experience is, mind you, that there's generally something at the bottom of what these country-folk hold to, and have held to for generations. But it's your drive' (or whatever it might have been: the golfing reader will have to imagine appropriate digressions at the proper intervals).

When conversation was resumed, Parkins said, with a slight hesitancy:

'A propos of what you were saying just now, Colonel, I think I ought to tell you that my own views on such subjects are very strong. I am, in fact, a convinced disbeliever in what is called the 'supernatural'.'

'What!' said the Colonel, 'do you mean to tell me you don't believe in second-sight, or ghosts, or anything of that kind?'

'In nothing whatever of that kind,' returned Parkins firmly.

'Well,' said the Colonel, 'but it appears to me at that rate, sir, that you must be little better than a Sadducee.'

Parkins was on the point of answering that, in his opinion, the Sadducees were the most sensible persons he had ever read of in the

Old Testament; but feeling some doubt as to whether much mention of them was to be found in that work, he preferred to laugh the accusation off.

'Perhaps I am,' he said; 'but — Here, give me my cleek, boy! — Excuse me one moment, Colonel.' A short interval. 'Now, as to whistling for the wind, let me give you my theory about it. The laws which govern winds are really not at all perfectly known — to fisherfolk and such, of course, not known at all. A man or woman of eccentric habits, perhaps, or a stranger, is seen repeatedly on the beach at some unusual hour, and is heard whistling. Soon afterwards a violent wind rises; a man who could read the sky perfectly or who possessed a barometer could have foretold that it would. The simple people of a fishing-village have no barometers, and only a few rough rules for prophesying weather. What more natural than that the eccentric personage I postulated should be regarded as having raised the wind, or that he or she should clutch eagerly at the reputation of being able to do so? Now, take last night's wind: as it happens, I myself was whistling. I blew a whistle twice, and the wind seemed to come absolutely in answer to my call. If anyone had seen me — '

The audience had been a little restive

under this harangue, and Parkins had, I fear, fallen somewhat into the tone of a lecturer; but at the last sentence the Colonel stopped.

'Whistling, were you?' he said. 'And what sort of whistle did you use? Play this stroke first.' Interval.

'About that whistle you were asking, Colonel. It's rather a curious one. I have it in my — No; I see I've left it in my room. As a matter of fact, I found it yesterday.'

And then Parkins narrated the manner of his discovery of the whistle, upon hearing which the Colonel grunted, and opined that, in Parkins's place, he should himself be careful about using a thing that had belonged to a set of Papists, of whom, speaking generally, it might be affirmed that you never knew what they might not have been up to. From this topic he diverged to the enormities of the Vicar, who had given notice on the previous Sunday that Friday would be the Feast of St Thomas the Apostle, and that there would be service at eleven o'clock in the church. This and other similar proceedings constituted in the Colonel's view a strong presumption that the Vicar was a concealed Papist, if not a Jesuit; and Parkins, who could not very readily follow the Colonel in this region, did not disagree with him. In fact, they got on so well together in the morning that there was not talk on either side of their separating after lunch.

Both continued to play well during the afternoon, or at least, well enough to make them forget everything else until the light began to fail them. Not until then did Parkins remember that he had meant to do some more investigating at the preceptory; but it was of no great importance, he reflected. One day was as good as another; he might as well go home with the Colonel.

As they turned the corner of the house, the Colonel was almost knocked down by a boy who rushed into him at the very top of his speed, and then, instead of running away, remained hanging on to him and panting. The first words of the warrior were naturally those of reproof and objurgation, but he very quickly discerned that the boy was almost speechless with fright. Inquiries were useless at first. When the boy got his breath he began to howl, and still clung to the Colonel's legs. He was at last detached, but continued to howl.

'What in the world is the matter with you? What have you been up to? What have you seen?' said the two men.

'Ow, I seen it wive at me out of the winder,' wailed the boy, 'and I don't like it.'

'What window?' said the irritated Colonel.

'Come pull yourself together, my boy.'

'The front winder it was, at the 'otel,' said the boy.

At this point Parkins was in favour of sending the boy home, but the Colonel refused; he wanted to get to the bottom of it, he said; it was most dangerous to give a boy such a fright as this one had had, and if it turned out that people had been playing jokes, they should suffer for it in some way. And by a series of questions he made out this story: The boy had been playing about on the grass in front of the Globe with some others; then they had gone home to their teas, and he was just going, when he happened to look up at the front winder and see it a-wiving at him. *It* seemed to be a figure of some sort, in white as far as he knew — couldn't see its face; but it wived at him, and it warn't a right thing — not to say not a right person. Was there a light in the room? No, he didn't think to look if there was a light. Which was the window? Was it the top one or the second one? The seckind one it was — the big winder what got two little uns at the sides.

'Very well, my boy,' said the Colonel, after a few more questions. 'You run away home now. I expect it was some person trying to give you a start. Another time, like a brave English boy, you just throw a stone — well, no, not that exactly, but you go and speak to the waiter, or to Mr Simpson, the landlord, and — yes — and say that I advised you to do so.'

The boy's face expressed some of the doubt he felt as to the likelihood of Mr Simpson's lending a favourable ear to his complaint, but the Colonel did not appear to perceive this, and went on:

'And here's a sixpence — no, I see it's a shilling — and you be off home, and don't think any more about it.'

The youth hurried off with agitated thanks, and the Colonel and Parkins went round to the front of the Globe and reconnoitred. There was only one window answering to the description they had been hearing.

'Well, that's curious,' said Parkins; 'it's evidently my window the lad was talking about. Will you come up for a moment, Colonel Wilson? We ought to be able to see if anyone has been taking liberties in my room.'

They were soon in the passage, and Parkins made as if to open the door. Then he stopped and felt in his pockets.

'This is more serious than I thought,' was his next remark. 'I remember now that before I started this morning I locked the door. It is locked now, and, what is more, here is the key.' And he held it up. 'Now,' he went on, 'if the servants are in the habit of going into one's room during the day when one is away, I can only say that — well, that I don't approve of it at all.' Conscious of a somewhat weak climax, he busied himself in opening the door (which was indeed locked) and in lighting candles. 'No,' he said, 'nothing seems disturbed.'

'Except your bed,' put in the Colonel.

'Excuse me, that isn't my bed,' said Parkins. 'I don't use that one. But it does look as if someone had been playing tricks with it.'

It certainly did: the clothes were bundled up and twisted together in a most tortuous confusion. Parkins pondered.

'That must be it,' he said at last. 'I disordered the clothes last night in unpacking, and they haven't made it since. Perhaps they came in to make it, and that boy saw them through the window; and then they were called away and locked the door after them. Yes, I think that must be it.'

'Well, ring and ask,' said the Colonel, and this appealed to Parkins as practical.

The maid appeared, and, to make a long story short, deposed that she had made the bed in the morning when the gentleman was in the room, and hadn't been there since. No, she hadn't no other key. Mr Simpson, he kep' the keys; he'd be able to tell the gentleman if anyone had been up.

This was a puzzle. Investigation showed that nothing of value had been taken, and Parkins remembered the disposition of the small objects on tables and so forth well enough to be pretty sure that no pranks had been played with them. Mr and Mrs Simpson furthermore agreed that neither of them had given the duplicate key of the room to any person whatever during the day. Nor could Parkins, fair-minded man as he was, detect anything in the demeanour of master, mistress, or maid that indicated guilt. He was much more inclined to think that the boy had been imposing on the Colonel.

The latter was unwontedly silent and pensive at dinner and throughout the evening. When he bade goodnight to Parkins, he murmured in a gruff undertone:

'You know where I am if you want me during the night.'

'Why, yes, thank you, Colonel Wilson, I think I do; but there isn't much prospect of my disturbing you, I hope. By the way,' he added, 'did I show you that old whistle I spoke of? I think not. Well, here it is.'

The Colonel turned it over gingerly in the light of the candle.

'Can you make anything of the inscription?' asked Parkins, as he took it back.

'No, not in this light. What do you mean to do with it?'

'Oh, well, when I get back to Cambridge I shall submit it to some of the archaeologists there, and see what they think of it; and very likely, if they consider it worth having, I may present it to one of the museums.'

'M!' said the Colonel. 'Well, you may be right. All I know is that, if it were mine, I should chuck it straight into the sea. It's no use talking, I'm well aware, but I expect that with you it's a case of live and learn. I hope so, I'm sure, and I wish you a good night.'

He turned away, leaving Parkins in act to speak at the bottom of the stair, and soon each was in his own bedroom.

By some unfortunate accident, there were neither blinds nor curtains to the windows of the Professor's room. The previous night he had thought little of this, but tonight there seemed every prospect of a bright moon rising to shine directly on his bed, and probably wake him later on. When he noticed this he was a good deal annoyed, but, with an ingenuity which I can only envy, he succeeded in rigging up, with the help of a railway-rug, some safety-pins, and a stick and umbrella, a screen which, if it only held together, would completely keep the moon-light off his bed. And shortly afterwards he was comfortably in that bed. When he had read a somewhat solid work long enough to produce a decided wish to sleep, he cast a drowsy glance round the room, blew out the candle, and fell back upon the pillow.

He must have slept soundly for an hour or more, when a sudden clatter shook him up in a most unwelcome manner. In a moment he realized what had happened: his carefully-constructed screen had given way, and a very bright frosty moon was shining directly on his face. This was highly annoying. Could he possibly get up and reconstruct the screen? or could he manage to sleep if he did not?

For some minutes he lay and pondered over all the possibilities; then he turned over sharply, and with his eyes open lay breathlessly listening. There had been a movement, he was sure, in the empty bed on the opposite side of the room. Tomorrow he would have it moved, for there must be rats or something playing about in it. It was quiet now. No! the commotion began again. There was a rustling and shaking: surely more than any rat could cause.

I can figure to myself something of the Professor's bewilderment and horror, for I have in a dream thirty years back seen the same thing happen; but the reader will hardly, perhaps, imagine how dreadful it was to him to see a figure suddenly sit up in what he had known was an empty bed. He was out of his own bed in one bound, and made a dash towards the window, where lay his only weapon, the stick with which he had propped his screen. This was, as it turned out, the worst thing he could have done, because the personage in the empty bed, with a sudden smooth motion, slipped from the bed and took up a position, with outspread arms, between the two beds, and in front of the door. Parkins watched it in a horrid perplexity. Somehow, the idea of getting past it and escaping through the door was intolerable to him; he could not have borne — he didn't know why — to touch it; and as for its touching him, he would sooner dash himself through the window than have that happen. It stood for the moment in a band of dark shadow, and he had not seen what its face was like. Now it began to move, in a stooping posture, and all at once the spectator realized, with some horror and some relief, that it must be blind, for it seemed to feel about it with its muffled arms in a groping and random fashion. Turning half away from him, it became suddenly conscious of the bed he had just left, and darted towards it, and bent and felt over the pillows in a way which made Parkins shudder as he had never in his life thought it possible. In a very few moments it seemed to know that the bed was empty, and then, moving forward into the area of light and facing the window, it showed for the first time what manner of thing it was.

Parkins, who very much dislikes being questioned about it, did once describe something of it in my hearing, and I gathered that what he chiefly remembers about it is a horrible, an intensely horrible, face *of crumpled linen*. What expression he read upon it he could not or would not tell, but that the fear of it went nigh to maddening him is certain.

But he was not at leisure to watch it for long. With formidable quickness it moved into the middle of the room, and, as it groped and waved, one corner of its draperies swept across Parkins's face. He could not, though he knew how perilous a sound was — he could not keep back a cry of disgust, and this gave the searcher an instant clue. It leapt towards him upon the instant, and the next moment he was half-way through the window backwards, uttering cry upon cry at the utmost pitch of his voice, and the linen face was thrust close into his own. At this, almost the last possible second, deliverance came, as you will have guessed: the Colonel burst the door open, and was just in time to see the dreadful group at the window. When he reached the figures only one was left. Parkins sank forward into the room in a faint, and before him on the floor lay a tumbled heap of bed-clothes.

Colonel Wilson asked no questions, but busied himself in keeping everyone else out of the room and in getting Parkins back to his bed; and himself, wrapped in a rug, occupied the other bed, for the rest of the night. Early on the next day Rogers arrived, more welcome than he would have been a day before, and the three of them held a very long consultation in the Professor's room. At the end of it the Colonel left the hotel door carrying a small object between his finger and thumb, which he cast as far into the sea as a very brawny arm could send it. Later on the smoke of a burning ascended from the back premises of the Globe.

Exactly what explanation was patched up for the staff and visitors at the hotel I must confess I do not recollect. The Professor was somehow cleared of the ready suspicion of delirium tremens, and the hotel of the reputation of a troubled house.

There is not much question as to what would have happened to Parkins if the Colonel had not intervened when he did. He would either have fallen out of the window or else lost his wits. But it is not so evident what more the creature that came in answer to the whistle could have done than frighten. There seemed to be absolutely nothing material about it save the bedclothes of which it had made itself a body. The Colonel, who remembered a not very dissimilar occurrence in India, was of the opinion that if Parkins had closed with it it could really have done very little, and that its one power was that of frightening. The whole thing, he said, served to confirm his opinion of the Church of Rome.

There is really nothing more to tell, but, as you may imagine, the Professor's views on certain points are less clear cut than they used to be. His nerves, too, have suffered: he cannot even now see a surplice hanging on a door quite unmoved, and the spectacle of a scarecrow in a field late on a winter afternoon has cost him more than one sleepless night.

LOT NO. 249

Sir Arthur Conan Doyle

Of the dealings of Edward Bellingham with William Monkhouse Lee, and of the cause of the great terror of Abercrombie Smith, it may be that no absolute and final judgment will ever be delivered. It is true that we have the full and clear narrative of Smith himself, and such corroboration as he could look for from Thomas Styles thc servant, from the Reverend Plumptree Peterson, Fellow of Old's, and from such other people as chanced to gain some passing glance at this or that incident in a singular chain of events. Yet, in the main, the story must rest upon Smith alone, and the most will think that it is more likely that one brain, however outwardly sane, has some subtle warp in its texture, some strange flaw in its workings, than that the path of Nature has been overstepped in open day in so famed a centre of learning and light as the University of Oxford. Yet when we think how narrow and how devious this path of Nature is, how dimly we can trace it, for all our lamps of science, and how from the darkness which girds it round great and terrible possibilities loom ever shadowly upwards, it is a bold and confident man who will put a limit to the strange by-paths into which the human spirit may wander.

In a certain wing of what we will call Old College in Oxford there is a corner turret of an exceeding great age. The heavy arch which spans the open door has bent downwards in the centre under the weight of its years, and the grey, lichen-blotched blocks of stone are bound and knitted together with withes and strands of ivy, as though the old mother had set herself to brace them up against wind and weather. From the door a stone stair curves upward spirally, passing two landings, and terminating in a third one, its steps all shapeless and hollowed by the tread of so many generations of the seekers after knowledge. Life has flowed like water down this winding stair, and, waterlike, has left these smooth-worn grooves behind it. From the long-gowned, pedantic scholars of Plantagenet days down to the young bloods of a later age, how full and strong has been that tide of young, English life. And what was left now of all those hopes, those strivings, those fiery energies, save here and there in some old-world churchyard a few scratches upon a stone, and perchance a handful of dust in a mouldering coffin? Yet here were the silent stair and the grey, old wall, with bend and saltire and many another heraldic device still to be read upon its surface, like grotesque shadows thrown back from the days that had passed.

In the month of May, in the year 1884, three young men occupied the sets of rooms which opened on to the separate landings of the old stair. Each set consisted simply of a sitting-room and of a bedroom, while the two corresponding rooms upon the ground-floor were used, the one as a coal-cellar, and the other as the living-room of the servant, or scout, Thomas Styles, whose duty it was to wait upon the three men above him. To right and to left was a line of lecture-rooms and of offices, so that the dwellers in the old turret enjoyed a certain seclusion, which made the chambers popular among the more studious undergraduates. Such were the three who occupied them now — Abercrombie Smith above, Edward Bellingham beneath him, and William Monkhouse Lee upon the lowest storey.

It was ten o'clock on a bright, spring night, and Abercrombie Smith lay back in his arm-chair, his feet upon the fender, and his briar-root pipe between his lips. In a similar chair, and equally at his ease, there lounged on the other side of the fireplace his old school friend Jephro Hastie. Both men were in flannels, for they had spent their evening upon the river, but apart from their dress no one could look at their hard-cut, alert faces without seeing that they were open-air men — men whose minds and tastes turned naturally to all that was manly and robust. Hastie, indeed, was stroke of his college boat, and Smith was an even better oar, but a coming examination had already cast its shadow over him and held him to his work, save for a few hours a week which health demanded. A litter of medical books upon the table, with scattered bones, models, and anatomical plates, pointed to the extent as well as the nature of his studies, while a couple of single-sticks and a set of boxing-gloves above the mantelpiece hinted at the means by which, with Hastie's help, he might take his exercise in its most compressed and least-distant form. They knew each other very well — so well that they could sit now in that soothing silence which is the very highest development of companionship.

'Have some whisky,' said Abercrombie Smith at last between two cloudbursts. 'Scotch in the jug and Irish in the bottle.'

'No, thanks. I'm in for the sculls. I don't liquor when I'm training. How about you?'

'I'm reading hard. I think it best to leave it alone.'

Hastie nodded, and they relapsed into a contented silence.

'By the way, Smith,' asked Hastie, presently, 'have you made the acquaintance of either of the fellows on your stair yet?'

'Just a nod when we pass. Nothing more.'

'Hum! I should be inclined to let it stand at that. I know something of them both. Not much, but as much as I want. I don't think I should take them to my bosom if I were you. Not that there's much amiss with Monkhouse Lee.'

'Meaning the thin one?'

'Precisely. He is a gentlemanly little fellow. I don't think there is any vice in him. But then you can't know him without knowing Bellingham.'

'Meaning the fat one?'

'Yes, the fat one. And he's a man whom I, for one, would rather not know.'

Abercrombie Smith raised his eyebrows and glanced across at his companion.

'What's up, then?' he asked. 'Drink? Cards? Cad? You used not to be censorious.'

'Ah! you evidently don't know the man, or you wouldn't ask. There's something damnable about him — something reptilian. My gorge always rises at him. I should put him down as a man with secret vices — an evil liver. He's no fool, though. They say that he is one of the best men in his line that they have ever had in the college.'

'Medicine or classics?'

'Eastern languages. He's a demon at them. Chillingworth met him somewhere above the second cataract last long, and he told me that he just prattled to the Arabs as if he had been born and nursed and weaned among them. He talked Coptic to the Copts, and Hebrew to the Jews, and Arabic to the Bedouins, and they were all ready to kiss the hem of his frock-coat. There are some old hermit Johnnies up in those parts who sit on rocks and scowl and spit at the casual stranger. Well, when they saw this chap Bellingham, before he had said five words they just lay down on their bellies and wriggled. Chillingworth said that he never saw anything like it. Bellingham seemed to take it as his right, too, and strutted about among them and talked down to them like a Dutch uncle. Pretty good for an undergrad. of Old's, wasn't it?'

'Why do you say you can't know Lee without knowing Bellingham?'

'Because Bellingham is engaged to his sister Eveline. Such a bright little girl, Smith! I know the whole family well. It's disgusting to see that brute with her. A toad and a dove, that's what they always remind me of.'

Abercrombie Smith grinned and knocked

his ashes out against the side of the grate.

'You show every card in your hand, old chap,' said he. 'What a prejudiced, green-eyed, evil-thinking old man it is! You have really nothing against the fellow except that.'

'Well, I've known her ever since she was as long as that cherry-wood pipe, and I don't like to see her taking risks. And it is a risk. He looks beastly. And he has a beastly temper, a venomous temper. You remember his row with Long Norton?'

'No; you always forget that I am a freshman.'

'Ah, it was last winter. Of course. Well, you know the towpath along by the river. There were several fellows going along it, Bellingham in front, when they came on an old market-woman coming the other way. It had been raining — you know what those fields are like when it has rained — and the path ran between the river and a great puddle that was nearly as broad. Well, what does this swine do but keep the path, and push the old girl into the mud, where she and her marketings came to terrible grief. It was a blackguard thing to do, and Long Norton, who is as gentle a fellow as ever stepped, told him what he thought of it. One word led to another, and it ended in Norton laying his stick across the fellow's shoulders. There was the deuce of a fuss about it, and it's a treat to see the way in which Bellingham looks at Norton when they meet now. By Jove, Smith, it's nearly eleven o'clock!'

'No hurry. Light your pipe again.'

'Not I. I'm supposed to be in training. Here I've been sitting gossiping when I ought to have been safely tucked up. I'll borrow your skull, if you can share it. Williams has had mine for a month. I'll take the little bones of your ear, too, if you are sure you won't need them. Thanks very much. Never mind a bag, I can carry them very well under my arm. Good night, my son, and take my tip as to your neighbour.'

When Hastie, bearing his anatomical plunder, had clattered off down the winding stair, Abercrombie Smith hurled his pipe into the wastepaper basket, and drawing his chair nearer to the lamp, plunged into a formidable, green-covered volume, adorned with great, coloured maps of that strange, internal kingdom of which we are the hapless and helpless monarchs. Though a freshman at Oxford, the student was not so in medicine, for he had worked for four years at Glasgow and at Berlin, and this coming examination would place him finally as a member of his profession. With his firm mouth, broad forehead, and clear-cut, somewhat hard-featured face, he was a man who, if he had no brilliant talent, was yet so dogged, so patient, and so strong that he might in the end overtop a more showy genius. A man who can hold his own among Scotchmen and North Germans is not a man to be easily set back. Smith had left a name at Glasgow and at Berlin, and he was bent now upon doing as much at Oxford, if hard work and devotion could accomplish it.

He had sat reading for about an hour, and the hands of the noisy carriage clock upon the side-table were rapidly closing together upon the twelve, when a sudden sound fell upon the student's ear — a sharp, rather shrill sound, like the hissing intake of a man's breath who gasps under some strong emotion. Smith laid down his book and slanted his ear to listen. There was no one on either side or above him, so that the interruption came certainly from the neighbour beneath — the same neighbour of whom Hastie had given so unsavoury an account. Smith knew him only as a flabby, pale-faced man of silent and studious habits, a man whose lamp threw a golden bar from the old turret even after he had extinguished his own. This community in lateness had formed a certain silent bond between them. It was soothing to Smith when the hours stole on towards dawning to feel that there was another so close who set as small a value upon his sleep as he did. Even now, as his thoughts turned towards him, Smith's feelings were kindly. Hastie was a good fellow, but he was rough, strong-fibred, with no imagination or sympathy. He could not tolerate departures from what he looked upon as the model type of manliness. If a man could not be measured by a public-school standard, then he was beyond the pale with Hastie. Like so many who are themselves robust, he was apt to confuse the constitution with the character, to ascribe to want of principle what was really a want of circulation. Smith, with his stronger mind, knew his friend's habit, and made allowance for it now as his thoughts turned towards the man beneath him.

There was no return of the singular sound, and Smith was about to turn to his work once more, when suddenly there broke out in the silence of the night a hoarse cry, a positive scream — the call of a man who is moved and shaken beyond all control. Smith sprang out of his chair and dropped his book. He was a man of fairly firm fibre, but there was something in this sudden, uncontrollable shriek of horror which chilled his blood and pringled in his skin. Coming in such a place and at such an hour, it brought a thousand fantastic possibilities into his head. Should he rush down, or was it better to wait? He had all the national hatred of making a scene, and he knew so little of his neighbour that he would not lightly intrude upon his affairs. For a moment he stood in doubt and even as he balanced the matter there was a quick rattle of footsteps upon the stairs, and young Monkhouse Lee, half-dressed and as white as ashes, burst into his room.

'Come down!' he gasped. 'Bellingham's ill.'

Abercrombie Smith followed him closely downstairs into the sitting-room which was beneath his own, and intent as he was upon the matter in hand, he could not but take an amazed glance around him as he crossed the threshold. It was such a chamber as he had never seen before — a museum rather than a study. Walls and ceiling were thickly covered with a thousand strange relics from Egypt and the East. Tall, angular figures bearing burdens or weapons stalked in an uncouth frieze round the apartments. Above were bull-headed, stork-headed, cat-headed, owl-headed statues, with viper-crowned, almond-eyed monarchs and strange, beetle-like deities cut out of the blue Egyptian lapis lazuli. Horus and Isis and Osiris peeped down from every niche and shelf, while across the ceiling a true son of Old Nile, a great, hanging-jawed crocodile, was slung in a double noose.

In the centre of this singular chamber was a large, square table, littered with papers, bottles, and the dried leaves of some graceful, palm-like plant. These varied objects had all been heaped together in order to make room for a mummy case, which had been conveyed from the wall, as was evident from the gap there, and laid across the front of the table. The mummy itself, a horrid, black, withered thing, like a charred head on a gnarled bush, was lying half out of the case, with its claw-like hand and bony forearm resting upon the table. Propped up against the sarcophagus was an old, yellow scroll of papyrus, and in front of it, in a wooden armchair, sat the owner of the room, his head thrown back, his widely opened eyes directed in a horrified stare to the crocodile above him, and his blue, thick lips puffing loudly with every expiration.

'My God! he's dying!' cried Monkhouse Lee, distractedly.

He was a slim, handsome young fellow, olive-skinned and dark-eyed, of a Spanish rather than of an English type, with a Celtic intensity of manner which contrasted with the Saxon phlegm of Abercrombie Smith.

'Only a faint, I think,' said the medical student. 'Just give me a hand with him. You take his feet. Now onto the sofa. Can you kick all those little wooden devils off? What a litter it is! Now he will be all right if we undo his collar and give him some water. What has he been up to at all?'

'I don't know. I heard him cry out. I ran up. I know him pretty well, you know. It is very good of you to come down.'

'His heart is going like a pair of castanets,' said Smith, laying his hand on the breast of the unconscious man. 'He seems to me to be frightened all to pieces. Chuck the water over him! What a face he has got on him!'

It was indeed a strange and most repellent face, for colour and outline were equally unnatural. It was white, not with the ordinary pallor of fear, but with an absolutely bloodless white, like the under side of a sole. He was very fat, but gave the impression of having at some time been considerably fatter, for his skin hung loosely in creases and folds, and was shot with a meshwork of wrinkles. Short, stubbly brown hair bristled up from his scalp, with a pair of thick, wrinkled ears protruding at the sides. His light-grey eyes were still open, the pupils dilated and the balls projecting in a fixed and horrid stare. It seemed to Smith as he looked down upon him that he had never seen Nature's danger signals flying so plainly upon a man's countenance, and his thoughts turned more seriously to the warning which Hastie had given him an hour before.

'What the deuce can have frightened him so?' he asked.

'It's the mummy.'

'The mummy? How, then?'

'I don't know. It's beastly and morbid. I wish he would drop it. It's the second fright he has given me. It was the same last winter. I found him just like this, with that horrid thing in front of him.'

'What does he want with the mummy, then?'

'Oh, he's a crank, you know. It's his hobby. He knows more about these things than any man in England. But I wish he wouldn't! Ah, he's beginning to come to.'

A faint tinge of colour had begun to steal back into Bellingham's ghastly cheeks, and his eyelids shivered like a sail after a calm. He clasped and unclasped his hands, drew a long, thin breath between his teeth, and suddenly jerking up his head, threw a glance of recognition around him. As his eyes fell upon the mummy, he sprang off the sofa, seized the roll of papyrus, thrust it into a drawer, turned the key, and staggered back on to the sofa.

'What's up?' he asked. 'What do you chaps want?'

'You've been shrieking out and making no end of a fuss,' said Monkhouse Lee. 'If our neighbour here from above hadn't come down, I'm sure I don't know what I should have done with you.'

'Ah, it's Abercrombie Smith,' said Bellingham, glancing up at him. 'How very good of you to come in! What a fool I am! Oh, my God, what a fool I am!'

He sank his head on to his hands, and burst into peal after peal of hysterical laughter.

'Look here! Drop it!' cried Smith, shaking him roughly by the shoulder.

'Your nerves are all in a jangle. You must drop these little midnight games with mummies, or you'll be going off your chump. You're all on wires now.'

'I wonder,' said Bellingham, 'whether you would be as cool as I am if you had seen — '

'What then?'

'Oh, nothing. I meant that I wonder if you could sit up at night with a mummy without trying your nerves. I have no doubt that you are quite right. I dare say that I have been taking it out of myself too much lately. But I am all right now. Please don't go, though. Just wait for a few minutes until I am quite myself.'

'The room is very close,' remarked Lee,

throwing open the window and letting in the cool night air.

'It's balsamic resin,' said Bellingham. He lifted up one of the dried palmate leaves from the table and frizzled it over the chimney of the lamp. It broke away into heavy smoke wreaths, and a pungent, biting odour filled the chamber. 'It's the sacred plant — the plant of the priests,' he remarked. 'Do you know anything of Eastern languages, Smith?'

'Nothing at all. Not a word.'

The answer seemed to lift a weight from the Egyptologist's mind.

'By the way,' he continued, 'how long was it from the time that you ran down, until I came to my senses?'

'Not long. Some four or five minutes.'

'I thought it could not be very long,' said he, drawing a long breath. 'But what a strange thing unconsciousness is! There is no measurement to it. I could not tell from my own sensations if it were seconds or weeks. Now that gentleman on the table was packed up in the days of the eleventh dynasty, some forty centuries ago, and yet if he could find his tongue, he would tell us that this lapse of time has been but a closing of the eyes and a reopening of them. He is a singularly fine mummy, Smith.'

Smith stepped over to the table and looked

down with a professional eye at the black and twisted form in front of him. The features, though horribly discoloured, were perfect, and two little nut-like eyes still lurked in the depths of the black, hollow sockets. The blotched skin was drawn tightly from bone to bone, and a tangled wrap of black, coarse hair fell over the ears. Two thin teeth, like those of a rat, overlay the shrivelled lower lip. In its crouching position, with bent joints and craned head, there was a suggestion of energy about the horrid thing which made Smith's gorge rise. The gaunt ribs, with their parchment-like covering, were exposed, and the sunken, leaden-hued abdomen, with the long slit where the embalmer had left his mark; but the lower limbs were wrapped round with coarse, yellow bandages. A number of little clove-like pieces of myrrh and of cassia were sprinkled over the body, and lay scattered on the inside of the case.

'I don't know his name,' said Bellingham, passing his hand over the shrivelled head. 'You see the outer sarcophagus with the inscriptions is missing. Lot 249 is all the title he has now. You see it printed on his case. That was his number in the auction at which I picked him up.'

'He has been a very pretty sort of fellow in his day,' remarked Abercrombie Smith.

'He has been a giant. His mummy is six feet seven in length, and that would be a giant over there, for they were never a very robust race. Feel these great, knotted bones, too. He would be a nasty fellow to tackle.'

'Perhaps these very hands helped to build the stones into the pyramids,' suggested Monkhouse Lee, looking down with disgust in his eyes at the crooked, unclean talons.

'No fear. This fellow has been pickled in natron, and looked after in the most approved style. They did not serve hodsmen in that fashion. Salt or bitumen was enough for them. It has been calculated that this sort of thing cost about seven hundred and thirty pounds in our money. Our friend was a noble at the least. What do you make of that small inscription near his feet, Smith?'

'I told you that I know no Eastern tongue.'

'Ah, so you did. It is the name of the embalmer, I take it. A very conscientious worker he must have been. I wonder how many modern works will survive four thousand years?'

He kept on speaking lightly and rapidly, but it was evident to Abercrombie Smith that he was still palpitating with fear. His hands shook, his lower lip trembled, and look where he would, his eye always came sliding round to his gruesome companion. Through all his fear, however, there was a suspicion of triumph in his tone and manner. His eyes shone, and his footstep, as he paced the room, was brisk and jaunty. He gave the impression of a man who has gone through an ordeal, the marks of which he still bears upon him, but which has helped him to his end.

'You're not going yet?' he cried, as Smith rose from the sofa.

At the prospect of solitude, his fears seemed to crowd back upon him, and he stretched out a hand to detain him.

'Yes, I must go. I have my work to do. You are all right now. I think that with your nervous system you should take up some less morbid study.'

'Oh, I am not nervous as a rule; and I have unwrapped mummies before.'

'You fainted last time,' observed Monkhouse Lee.

'Ah, yes, so I did. Well, I must have a nerve tonic or a course of electricity. You are not going, Lee?'

'I'll do whatever you wish, Ned.'

'Then I'll come down with you and have a shakedown on your sofa. Good night, Smith. I am so sorry to have disturbed you with my foolishness.'

They shook hands, and as the medical

student stumbled up the spiral and irregular stair he heard a key turn in a door, and the steps of his two new acquaintances as they descended to the lower floor.

In this strange way began the acquaintance between Edward Bellingham and Abercrombie Smith, an acquaintance which the latter, at least, had no desire to push further. Bellingham, however, appeared to have taken a fancy to his rough-spoken neighbour, and made his advances in such a way that he could hardly be repulsed without absolute brutality. Twice he called to thank Smith for his assistance, and many times afterwards he looked in with books, papers and such other civilities as two bachelor neighbours can offer each other. He was, as Smith soon found, a man of wide reading, with catholic tastes and an extraordinary memory. His manner, too, was so pleasing and suave that one came, after a time, to overlook his repellent appearance. For a jaded and wearied man he was no unpleasant companion, and Smith found himself, after a time, looking forward to his visits, and even returning them.

Clever as he undoubtedly was, however, the medical student seemed to detect a dash of insanity in the man. He broke out at times into a high, inflated style of talk which was in contrast with the simplicity of his life.

‘It is a wonderful thing,’ he cried,’ to feel that one can command powers of good and of evil — a ministering angel or a demon of vengeance.’ And again, of Monkhouse Lee, he said, — ‘Lee is a good fellow, an honest fellow, but he is without strength or ambition. He would not make a fit partner for a man with a great enterprise. He would not make a fit partner for me.’

At such hints and innuendoes stolid Smith, puffing solemnly at his pipe, would simply raise his eyebrows and shake his head, with little interjections of medical wisdom as to earlier hours and fresher air.

One habit Bellingham had developed of late which Smith knew to be a frequent herald of a weakening mind. He appeared to be for ever talking to himself. At late hours of the night, when there could be no visitor with him, Smith could still hear his voice beneath him in a low, muffled monologue, sunk almost to a whisper, and yet very audible in the silence. This solitary babbling annoyed and distracted the student, so that he spoke more than once to his neighbour about it. Bellingham, however, flushed up at the charge, and denied curtly that he had uttered a sound; indeed, he showed more annoyance over the matter than the occasion seemed to demand.

Had Abercrombie Smith had any doubt as to his own ears he had not to go far to find corroboration. Tom Styles, the little wrinkled man-servant who had attended to the wants of the lodgers in the turret for a longer time than any man's memory could carry him, was sorely put to it over the same matter.

'If you please, sir,' said he, as he tidied down the top chamber one morning, 'do you think Mr. Bellingham is all right, sir?'

'All right, Styles?'

'Yes, sir. Right in the head, sir.'

'Why should he not be, then?'

'Well, I don't know, sir. His habits has changed of late. He's not the same man he used to be, though I make free to say that he was never quite one of my gentlemen, like Mr. Hastie or yourself, sir. He's took to talkin' to himself something awful. I wonder it don't disturb you. I don't know what to make of him, sir.'

'I don't know what business it is of yours, Styles.'

'Well, I takes an interest, Mr. Smith. It may be forward of me, but I can't help it. I feel sometimes as if I was mother and father to my young gentlemen. It all falls on me when things go wrong and the relations come. But Mr. Bellingham, sir. I want to know what it is that walks about his room sometimes when he's out and when the door's locked on the outside.'

'Eh? you're talking nonsense, Styles.'

'Maybe so, sir; but I heard it more'n once with my own ears.'

'Rubbish, Styles.'

'Very good, sir. You'll ring the bell if you want me.'

Abercrombie Smith gave little heed to the gossip of the old man-servant, but a small incident occurred a few days later which left an unpleasant effect upon his mind, and brought the words of Styles forcibly to his memory.

Bellingham had come up to see him late one night, and was entertaining him with an interesting account of the rock tombs of Beni Hassan in Upper Egypt, when Smith, whose hearing was remarkably acute, distinctly heard the sound of a door opening on the landing below.

'There's some fellow gone in or out of your room,' he remarked.

Bellingham sprang up and stood helpless for a moment, with the expression of a man who is half-incredulous and half-afraid.

'I surely locked it. I am almost positive that I locked it,' he stammered. 'No one could have opened it.'

'Why, I hear someone coming up the steps now,' said Smith.

Bellingham rushed out through the door, slammed it loudly behind him, and hurried down the stairs. About half-way down Smith heard him stop, and thought he caught the sound of whispering. A moment later the door beneath him shut, a key creaked in a lock, and Bellingham, with beads of moisture upon his pale face, ascended the stairs once more, and re-entered the room.

'It's all right,' he said, throwing himself down in a chair. 'It was that fool of a dog. He had pushed the door open. I don't know how I came to forget to lock it.'

'I didn't know you kept a dog,' said Smith, looking very thoughtfully at the disturbed face of his companion.

'Yes, I haven't had him long. I must get rid of him. He's a great nuisance.'

'He must be, if you find it so hard to shut him up. I should have thought that shutting the door would have been enough, without locking it.'

'I want to prevent old Styles from letting him out. He's of some value, you know, and it would be awkward to lose him.'

'I am a bit of a dog-fancier myself,' said Smith, still gazing hard at his companion from the corner of his eyes. 'Perhaps you'll let me have a look at it.'

'Certainly. But I am afraid it cannot be

to-night; I have an appointment. Is that clock right? Then I am a quarter of an hour late already. You'll excuse me, I am sure.'

He picked up his cap and hurried from the room. In spite of his appointment, Smith heard him re-enter his own chamber and lock his door upon the inside.

This interview left a disagreeable impression upon the medical student's mind. Bellingham had lied to him, and lied so clumsily that it looked as if he had desperate reasons for concealing the truth. Smith knew that his neighbour had no dog. He knew, also, that the step which he had heard upon the stairs was not the step of an animal. But if it were not, then what could it be? There was old Style's statement about the something which used to pace the room at times when the owner was absent. Could it be a woman? Smith rather inclined to the view. If so, it would mean disgrace and expulsion to Bellingham if it were discovered by the authorities, so that his anxiety and falsehoods might be accounted for. And yet it was inconceivable that an undergraduate could keep a woman in his rooms without being instantly detected. Be the explanation what it might, there was something ugly about it, and Smith determined, as he turned to his books, to discourage all further attempts at intimacy on the part of his soft-spoken and ill-favoured neighbour.

But his work was destined to interruption that night. He had hardly caught up the broken threads when a firm, heavy footfall came three steps at a time from below, and Hastie, in blazer and flannels, burst into the room.

'Still at it!' said he, plumping down into his wonted arm-chair. 'What a chap you are to stew! I believe an earthquake might come and knock Oxford into a cocked hat, and you would sit perfectly placid with your books among the ruins. However, I won't bore you long. Three whiffs of baccy, and I am off.'

'What's the news, then?' asked Smith, cramming a plug of bird's-eye into his briar with his forefinger.

'Nothing very much. Wilson made 70 for the freshmen against the eleven. They say that they will play him instead of Buddicomb, for Buddicomb is clean off colour. He used to be able to bowl a little, but it's nothing but half-volleys and long hops now.'

'Medium right,' suggested Smith, with the intense gravity which comes upon a 'varsity man when he speaks of athletics.

'Inclining to fast, with a work from leg. Comes with the arm about three inches or so. He used to be nasty on a wet wicket. Oh, by the way, have you heard about Long Norton?'

'What's that?'

'He's been attacked.'

'Attacked?'

'Yes, just as he was turning out of the High Street, and within a hundred yards of the gate of Old's.'

'But who — '

'Ah, that's the rub! If you said 'what,' you would be more grammatical. Norton swears that it was not human, and, indeed, from the scratches on his throat, I should be inclined to agree with him.'

'What, then? Have we come down to spooks?'

Abercrombie Smith puffed his scientific contempt.

'Well, no; I don't think that is quite the idea, either. I am inclined to think that if any showman has lost a great ape lately, and the brute is in these parts, a jury would find a true bill against it. Norton passes that way every night, you know, about the same hour. There's a tree that hangs low over the path — the big elm from Rainy's garden. Norton thinks the thing dropped on him out of the tree. Anyhow, he was nearly strangled by two arms, which, he says, were as strong and as thin as steel bands. He saw nothing; only those beastly arms that tightened and tightened on him. He yelled his head nearly off, and a couple of chaps came running, and the thing went over the wall like a cat. He never got a fair sight of it the whole time. It gave Norton a shake up, I can tell you. I tell him it has been as good as a change at the seaside for him.'

'A garrotter, most likely,' said Smith.

'Very possibly. Norton says not; but we don't mind what he says. The garrotter had long nails, and was pretty smart at swinging himself over walls. By the way, your beautiful neighbour would be pleased if he heard about it. He had a grudge against Norton, and he's not a man, from what I know of him, to forget his little debts. But hallo, old chap, what have you got in your noddle?'

'Nothing,' Smith answered, curtly.

He had started in his chair, and the look had flashed over his face which comes upon a man who is struck suddenly by some unpleasant idea.

'You looked as if something I had said had taken you on the raw. By the way, you have made the acquaintance of Master B. since I looked in last, have you not? Young Monkhouse Lee told me something to that effect.'

'Yes; I know him slightly. He has been up here once or twice.'

'Well, you're big enough and ugly enough to take care of yourself. He's not what I should call exactly a healthy sort of Johnny, though, no doubt, he's very clever, and all that. But you'll soon find out for yourself. Lee is all right; he's a very decent little fellow. Well, so long, old chap! I row Mullins for the Vice-Chancellor's pot on Wednesday week, so mind you come down, in case I don't see you before.'

Bovine Smith laid down his pipe and turned stolidly to his books once more. But with all the will in the world, he found it very hard to keep his mind upon his work. It would slip away to brood upon the man beneath him, and upon the little mystery which hung round his chambers. Then his thoughts turned to this singular attack of which Hastie had spoken, and to the grudge which Bellingham was said to owe to the object of it. The two ideas would persist in rising together in his mind, as though there were some close and intimate connection between them. And yet the suspicion was so dim and vague that it could not be put down in words.

'Confound the chap!' cried Smith, as he shied his book on pathology across the room. 'He has spoiled my night's reading, and that's reason enough, if there were no other, why I should steer clear of him in the future.'

For ten days the medical student confined himself so closely to his studies that he neither saw nor heard anything of either of the men beneath him. At the hours when Bellingham had been accustomed to visit him, he took care to sport his oak, and though he more than once heard a knocking at his outer door, he resolutely refused to answer it. One afternoon, however, he was descending the stairs when, just as he was passing it, Bellingham's door flew open, and young Monkhouse Lee came out with his eyes sparkling and a dark flush of anger upon his olive cheeks. Close at his heels followed Bellingham, his fat, unhealthy face all quivering with malignant passion.

'You fool!' he hissed. 'You'll be sorry.'

'Very likely,' cried the other. 'Mind what I say. It's off! I won't hear of it!'

'You've promised, anyhow.'

'Oh, I'll keep that! I won't speak. But I'd rather little Eva was in her grave. Once for all, it's off. She'll do what I say. We don't want to see you again.'

So much Smith could not avoid hearing, but he hurried on, for he had no wish to be involved in their dispute. There had been a serious breach between them, that was clear enough, and Lee was going to cause the engagement with his sister to be broken off. Smith thought of Hastie's comparison of the toad and the dove, and was glad to think that the matter was at an end. Bellingham's face when he was in a passion was not pleasant to look upon. He was not a man to whom an innocent girl could be trusted for life. As he walked, Smith wondered languidly what could have caused the quarrel, and what the promise might be which Bellingham had been so anxious that Monkhouse Lee should keep.

It was the day of the sculling match between Hastie and Mullins, and a stream of men were making their way down to the banks of the Isis. A May sun was shining brightly, and the yellow path was barred with the black shadows of tall elm-trees. On either side the grey colleges lay back from the road, the hoary old mothers of minds looking out from their high, mullioned windows at the tide of young life which swept so merrily past them. Black-clad tutors, prim officials, pale, reading men, brown-faced, straw-hatted young athletes in white sweaters or many-coloured blazers, all were hurrying towards the blue, winding river which curves through the Oxford meadows.

Abercrombie Smith, with the intuition of an old oarsman, chose his position at the point where he knew that the struggle, if there were a struggle, would come. Far off he heard the hum which announced the start, the gathering roar of the approach, the thunder of running feet, and the shouts of the men in the boats beneath him. A spray of half-clad, deep-breathing runners shot past him, and craning over their shoulders, he saw Hastie pulling a steady thirty-six, while his opponent, with a jerky forty, was a good boat's length behind him. Smith gave a cheer for his friend, and pulling out his watch, was starting off again for his chambers, when he felt a touch upon his shoulder, and found that young Monkhouse Lee was beside him.

'I saw you there,' he said, in a timid, deprecating way. 'I wanted to speak to you, if you could spare me a half-hour. This cottage is mine. I share it with Harrington of King's. Come in and have a cup of tea.'

'I must be back presently,' said Smith. 'I am hard on the grind at present. But I'll come in for a few minutes with pleasure. I wouldn't have come out only Hastie is a friend of mine.'

'So he is of mine. Hasn't he a beautiful style? Mullins wasn't in it. But come into the cottage. It's a little den of a place, but it is pleasant to work in during the summer months.'

It was a small, square, white building, with

green doors and shutters, and a rustic trellis-work porch, standing back some fifty yards from the river's bank. Inside, the main room was roughly fitted up as a study — deal table, unpainted shelves with books, and a few cheap oleographs upon the wall. A kettle sang upon a spirit-stove, and there were tea things upon a tray on the table.

'Try that chair and have a cigarette,' said Lee. 'Let me pour you out a cup of tea. It's so good of you to come in, for I know that your time is a good deal taken up. I wanted to say to you that, if I were you, I should change my rooms at once.'

'Eh?'

Smith sat staring at a lighted match in one hand and his unlit cigarette in the other.

'Yes; it must seem very extraordinary, and the worst of it is that I cannot give my reasons, for I am under a solemn promise — a very solemn promise. But I may go so far as to say that I don't think Bellingham is a very safe man to live near. I intend to camp out here as much as I can for a time.'

'Not safe! What do you mean?'

'Ah, that's what I mustn't say. But do take my advice and move your rooms. We had a grand row to-day. You must have heard us, for you came down the stairs.'

'I saw that you had fallen out.'

‘He’s a horrible chap, Smith. That is the only word for him. I have had doubts about him ever since that night when he fainted — you remember, when you came down. I taxed him to-day, and he told me things that made my hair rise, and wanted me to stand in with him. I’m not straight-laced, but I am a clergyman’s son, you know, and I think there are some things which are quite beyond the pale. I only thank God that I found him out before it was too late, for he was to have married into my family.’

‘This is all very fine, Lee,’ said Abercrombie Smith curtly. ‘But either you are saying a great deal too much or a great deal too little.’

‘I give you a warning.’

‘If there is real reason for warning, no promise can bind you. If I see a rascal about to blow a place up with dynamite no pledge will stand in my way of preventing him.’

‘Ah, but I cannot prevent him, and I can do nothing but warn you.’

‘Without saying what you warn me against.’

‘Against Bellingham.’

‘But that is childish. Why should I fear him, or any man?’

‘I can’t tell you. I can only entreat you to change your rooms. You are in danger where you are. I don’t even say that Bellingham would wish to injure you. But it might happen, for he is a dangerous neighbour just now.'

'Perhaps I know more than you think,' said Smith, looking keenly at the young man's boyish, earnest face. 'Suppose I tell you that someone else shares Bellingham's rooms.'

Monkhouse Lee sprang from his chair in uncontrollable excitement.

'You know, then?' he gasped.

'A woman.'

Lee dropped back again with a groan.

'My lips are sealed,' he said. 'I must not speak.'

'Well, anyhow,' said Smith, rising, 'it is not likely that I should allow myself to be frightened out of rooms which suit me very nicely. It would be a little too feeble for me to move out all my goods and chattels because you say that Bellingham might in some unexplained way do me an injury. I think that I'll just take my chance, and stay where I am, and as I see that it's nearly five o'clock, I must ask you to excuse me.'

He bade the young student adieu in a few curt words, and made his way homeward through the sweet spring evening, feeling half-ruffled, half-amused, as any other strong, unimaginative man might who has been menaced by a vague and shadowy danger.

There was one little indulgence which Abercrombie Smith always allowed himself, however closely his work might press upon him. Twice a week, on the Tuesday and the Friday, it was his invariable custom to walk over to Farlingford, the residence of Doctor Plumptree Peterson, situated about a mile and a half out of Oxford. Peterson had been a close friend of Smith's elder brother, Francis, and as he was a bachelor, fairly well-to-do, with a good cellar and a better library, his house was a pleasant goal for a man who was in need of a brisk walk. Twice a week, then, the medical student would swing out there along the dark country roads and spend a pleasant hour in Peterson's comfortable study, discussing, over a glass of old port, the gossip of the 'varsity or the latest developments of medicine or of surgery.

On the day which followed his interview with Monkhouse Lee, Smith shut up his books at a quarter past eight, the hour when he usually started for his friend's house. As he was leaving his room, however, his eyes chanced to fall upon one of the books which Bellingham had lent him, and his conscience pricked him for not having returned it. However repellent the man might be, he should not be treated with discourtesy. Taking the book, he walked downstairs and knocked at his neighbour's door. There was no answer; but on turning the handle he found that it was unlocked. Pleased at the thought of avoiding an interview, he stepped inside, and placed the book with his card upon the table.

The lamp was turned half down, but Smith could see the details of the room plainly enough. It was all much as he had seen it before — the frieze, the animal-headed gods, the hanging crocodile, and the table littered over with papers and dried leaves. The mummy case stood upright against the wall, but the mummy itself was missing. There was no sign of any second occupant of the room, and he felt as he withdrew that he had probably done Bellingham an injustice. Had he a guilty secret to preserve, he would hardly leave his door open so that all the world might enter.

The spiral stair was as black as pitch, and Smith was slowly making his way down its irregular steps, when he was suddenly conscious that something had passed him in the darkness. There was a faint sound, a whiff of air, a light brushing past his elbow, but so slight that he could scarcely be certain of it. He stopped and listened, but the wind was rustling among the ivy outside, and he could hear nothing else.

'Is that you, Styles?' he shouted.

There was no answer, and all was still behind him. It must have been a sudden gust of air, for there were crannies and cracks in the old turret. And yet he could almost have sworn that he heard a footfall by his very side. He had emerged into the quadrangle, still turning the matter over in his head, when a man came running swiftly across the smooth-cropped lawn.

'Is that you, Smith?'

'Hullo, Hastie!'

'For God's sake come at once! Young Lee is drowned! Here's Harrington of King's with the news. The doctor is out. You'll do, but come along at once. There may be life in him.'

'Have you brandy?'

'No.'

'I'll bring some. There's a flask on my table.'

Smith bounded up the stairs, taking three at a time, seized the flask, and was rushing down with it, when, as he passed Bellingham's room, his eyes fell upon something which left him gasping and staring upon the landing.

The door, which he had closed behind him, was now open, and right in front of him, with the lamp-light shining upon it, was the mummy case. Three minutes ago it had been empty. He could swear to that. Now it framed the lank body of its horrible occupant, who stood, grim and stark, with his black, shrivelled face towards the door. The form was lifeless and inert, but it seemed to Smith as he gazed that there still lingered a lurid spark of vitality, some faint sign of consciousness in the little eyes which lurked in the depths of the hollow sockets. So astounded and shaken was he that he had forgotten his errand, and was still staring at the lean, sunken figure when the voice of his friend below recalled him to himself.

'Come on, Smith!' he shouted. 'It's life and death, you know. Hurry up! Now, then,' he added, as the medical student reappeared, 'let us do a sprint. It is well under a mile, and we should do it in five minutes. A human life is better worth running for than a pot.'

Neck and neck they dashed through the darkness, and did not pull up until panting and spent, they had reached the little cottage by the river. Young Lee, limp and dripping like a broken water-plant, was stretched upon the sofa, the green scum of the river upon his black hair, and a fringe of white foam upon his leaden-hued lips. Beside him knelt his fellow-student, Harrington, endeavouring to chafe some warmth back into his rigid limbs.

'I think there's life in him,' said Smith, with

his hand to the lad's side. 'Put your watch glass to his lips. Yes, there's dimming on it. You take one arm, Hastie. Now work it as I do, and we'll soon pull him round.'

For ten minutes they worked in silence, inflating and depressing the chest of the unconscious man. At the end of that time a shiver ran through his body, his lips trembled, and he opened his eyes. The three students burst out into an irrepressible cheer.

'Wake up, old chap. You've frightened us quite enough.'

'Have some brandy. Take a sip from the flask.'

'He's all right now,' said his companion Harrington. 'Heavens, what a fright I got! I was reading here, and he had gone out for a stroll as far as the river, when I heard a scream and a splash. Out I ran, and by the time I could find him and fish him out, all life seemed to have gone. Then Simpson couldn't get a doctor, for he has a game-leg, and I had to run, and I don't know what I'd have done without you fellows. That's right, old chap. Sit up.'

Monkhouse Lee had raised himself on his hands, and looked wildly about him.

'What's up?' he asked. 'I've been in the water. Ah, yes; I remember.'

A look of fear came into his eyes, and he

sank his face into his hands.

'How did you fall in?'

'I didn't fall in.'

'How then?'

'I was thrown in. I was standing by the bank, and something from behind picked me up like a feather and hurled me in. I heard nothing, and I saw nothing. But I know what it was, for all that.'

'And so do I,' whispered Smith.

Lee looked up with a quick glance of surprise.

'You've learned, then?' he said. 'You remember the advice I gave you?'

'Yes, and I begin to think that I shall take it.'

'I don't know what the deuce you fellows are talking about,' said Hastie, 'but I think, if I were you, Harrington, I should get Lee to bed at once. It will be time enough to discuss the why and the wherefore when he is a little stronger. I think, Smith, you and I can leave him alone now. I am walking back to college; if you are coming in that direction, we can have a chat.'

But it was little chat that they had upon their homeward path. Smith's mind was too full of the incidents of the evening, the absence of the mummy from his neighbour's rooms, the step that passed him on the stair, the reappearance — the extraordinary, inexplicable reappearance of the grisly thing — and then this attack upon Lee, corresponding so closely to the previous outrage upon another man against whom Bellingham bore a grudge. All this settled in his thoughts, together with the many little incidents which had previously turned him against his neighbour, and the singular circumstances under which he was first called in to him. What had been a dim suspicion, a vague, fantastic conjecture, had suddenly taken form, and stood out in his mind as a grim fact, a thing not to be denied. And yet, how monstrous it was! how unheard of! how entirely beyond all bounds of human experience. An impartial judge, or even the friend who walked by his side, would simply tell him that his eyes had deceived him, that the mummy had been there all the time, that young Lee had tumbled into the river as any other man tumbles into a river, and the blue pill was the best thing for a disordered liver. He felt that he would have said as much if the positions had been reversed. And yet he could swear that Bellingham was a murderer at heart, and that he wielded a weapon such as no man had ever used in all the grim history of crime.

Hastie had branched off to his rooms with

a few crisp and emphatic comments upon his friend's unsociability, and Abercrombie Smith crossed the quadrangle to his corner turret with a strong feeling of repulsion for his chambers and their associations. He would take Lee's advice, and move his quarters as soon as possible, for how could a man study when his ear was ever straining for every murmur or footstep in the room below? He observed, as he crossed over the lawn, that the light was still shining in Bellingham's window, and as he passed up the staircase the door opened, and the man himself looked out at him. With his fat, evil face he was like some bloated spider fresh from the weaving of his poisonous web.

'Good evening,' said he. 'Won't you come in?'

'No,' cried Smith fiercely.

'No? You are as busy as ever? I wanted to ask you about Lee. I was sorry to hear that there was a rumour that something was amiss with him.'

His features were grave, but there was the gleam of a hidden laugh in his eyes as he spoke. Smith saw it, and he could have knocked him down for it.

'You'll be sorrier still to hear that Monkhouse Lee is doing very well, and is out of all danger,' he answered. 'Your hellish tricks have not come off this time. Oh, you needn't try to brazen it out. I know all about it.'

Bellingham took a step back from the angry student, and half-closed the door as if to protect himself.

'You are mad,' he said. 'What do you mean? Do you assert that I had anything to do with Lee's accident?'

'Yes,' thundered Smith. 'You and that bag of bones behind you; you worked it between you. I tell you what it is, Master B., they have given up burning folk like you, but we still keep a hangman, and, by George! if any man in this college meets his death while you are here, I'll have you up, and if you don't swing for it, it won't be my fault. You'll find that your filthy Egyptian tricks won't answer in England.'

'You're a raving lunatic,' said Bellingham.

'All right. You just remember what I say, for you'll find that I'll be better than my word.'

The door slammed, and Smith went fuming up to his chamber, where he locked the door upon the inside, and spent half the night in smoking his old briar and brooding over the strange events of the evening.

Next morning Abercrombie Smith heard nothing of his neighbour, but Harrington called upon him in the afternoon to say that Lee was almost himself again. All day Smith stuck fast to his work, but in the evening he determined to pay the visit to his friend Doctor Peterson upon which he had started the night before. A good walk and a friendly chat would be welcome to his jangled nerves.

Bellingham's door was shut as he passed, but glancing back when he was some distance from the turret, he saw his neighbour's head at the window outlined against the lamp-light, his face pressed apparently against the glass as he gazed out into the darkness. It was a blessing to be away from all contact with him, if but for a few hours, and Smith stepped out briskly, and breathed the soft spring air into his lungs. The half-moon lay in the west between two Gothic pinnacles, and threw upon the silvered street a dark tracery from the stonework above. There was a brisk breeze, and light, fleecy clouds drifted swiftly across the sky. Old's was on the very border of the town, and in five minutes Smith found himself beyond the houses and between the hedges of a May-scented, Oxfordshire lane.

It was a lonely and little-frequented road which led to his friend's house. Early as it was, Smith did not meet a single soul upon his way. He walked briskly along until he came to the avenue gate, which opened into the long, gravel drive leading up to Farlingford. In front of him he could see the cosy, red light of the windows glimmering through the foliage. He stood with his hand upon the iron latch of the swinging gate, and he glanced back at the road along which he had come. Something was coming swiftly down it.

It moved in the shadow of the hedge, silently and furtively, a dark, crouching figure, dimly visible against the black background. Even as he gazed back at it, it had lessened its distance by twenty paces, and was fast closing upon him. Out of the darkness he had a glimpse of a scraggy neck, and of two eyes that will ever haunt him in his dreams. He turned, and with a cry of terror he ran for his life up the avenue. There were the red lights, the signals of safety, almost within a stone's-throw of him. He was a famous runner, but never had he run as he ran that night.

The heavy gate had swung into place behind him but he heard it dash open again before his pursuer. As he rushed madly and wildly through the night, he could hear a swift, dry patter behind him, and could see, as he threw back a glance, that this horror was bounding like a tiger at his heels, with blazing eyes and one stringy arm out-thrown.

Thank God, the door was ajar. He could see the thin bar of light which shot from the lamp in the hall. Nearer yet sounded the clatter from behind. He heard a hoarse gurgling at his very shoulder. With a shriek he flung himself against the door, slammed and bolted it behind him, and sank half-fainting on to the hall chair.

'My goodness, Smith, what's the matter?' asked Peterson, appearing at the door of his study.

'Give me some brandy.'

Peterson disappeared, and came rushing out again with a glass and a decanter.

'You need it,' he said, as his visitor drank off what he poured out for him. 'Why, man, you are as white as a cheese.'

Smith laid down his glass, rose up, and took a deep breath.

'I am my own man again now,' said he. 'I was never so unmanned before. But, with your leave, Peterson, I will sleep here to-night, for I don't think I could face that road again except by daylight. It's weak, I know, but I can't help it.'

Peterson looked at his visitor with a very questioning eye.

'Of course you shall sleep here if you wish. I'll tell Mrs. Burney to make up the spare bed. Where are you off to now?'

'Come up with me to the window that overlooks the door. I want you to see what I have seen.'

They went up to the window of the upper hall whence they could look down upon the approach to the house. The drive and the fields on either side lay quiet and still, bathed in the peaceful moonlight.

'Well, really, Smith,' remarked Peterson, 'it is well that I know you to be an abstemious man. What in the world can have frightened you?'

'I'll tell you presently. But where can it have gone? Ah, now, look, look! See the curve of the road just beyond your gate.'

'Yes, I see; you needn't pinch my arm off. I saw someone pass. I should say a man, rather thin, apparently, and tall, very tall. But what of him? And what of yourself? You are still shaking like an aspen leaf.'

'I have been within hand-grip of the devil, that's all. But come down to your study, and I shall tell you the whole story.'

He did so. Under the cheery lamp-light with a glass of wine on the table beside him, and the portly form and florid face of his friend in front, he narrated, in their order, all the events, great and small, which had formed so singular a chain, from the night on which he had found Bellingham fainting in front of the mummy case until this horrid experience of an hour ago.

'There now,' he said as he concluded, 'that's the whole, black business. It is monstrous and incredible, but it is true.'

Doctor Plumptree Peterson sat for some time in silence with a very puzzled expression upon his face.

'I never heard of such a thing in my life, never!' he said at last. 'You have told me the facts. Now tell me your inferences.'

'You can draw your own.'

'But I should like to hear yours. You have thought over the matter, and I have not.'

'Well, it must be a little vague in detail, but the main points seem to me to be clear enough. This fellow Bellingham, in his Eastern studies, has got hold of some infernal secret by which a mummy — or possibly only this particular mummy — can be temporarily brought to life. He was trying this disgusting business on the night when he fainted. No doubt the sight of the creature moving had shaken his nerve, even though he had expected it. You remember that almost the first words he said were to call out upon himself as a fool. Well, he got more hardened afterwards, and carried the matter through without fainting. The vitality which he could put into it was evidently only a passing thing, for I have seen it continually in its case as dead as this table. He has some elaborate process, I fancy, by which he brings the thing to pass. Having done it, he naturally bethought him that he might use the creature as an agent. It has intelligence and it has strength. For some purpose he took Lee into his confidence; but Lee, like a decent Christian, would have nothing to do with such a business. Then they had a row, and Lee vowed that he would tell his sister of Bellingham's true character. Bellingham's game was to prevent him, and he nearly managed it, by setting this creature of his on his track. He had already tried its powers upon another man — Norton — towards whom he had a grudge. It is the merest chance that he has not two murders upon his soul. Then, when I taxed him with the matter, he had the strongest reasons for wishing to get me out of the way before I could convey my knowledge to anyone else. He got his chance when I went out, for he knew my habits and where I was bound for. I have had a narrow shave, Peterson, and it is mere luck that you didn't find me on your doorstep in the morning. I'm not a nervous man as a rule, and I never thought to have the fear of death put upon me as it was to-night.'

'My dear boy, you take the matter too

seriously,' said his companion. 'Your nerves are out of order with your work, and you make too much of it. How could such a thing as this stride about the streets of Oxford, even at night, without being seen?'

'It has been seen. There is quite a scare in the town about an escaped ape, as they imagine the creature to be. It is the talk of the place.'

'Well, it's a striking chain of events. And yet, my dear fellow, you must allow that each incident in itself is capable of a more natural explanation?'

'What! even my adventure of to-night?'

'Certainly. You come out with your nerves all unstrung, and your head full of this theory of yours. Some gaunt, half-famished tramp steals after you, and seeing you run, is emboldened to pursue you. Your fears and imagination do the rest.'

'It won't do, Peterson; it won't do.'

'And again, in the instance of your finding the mummy case empty, and then a few moments later with an occupant, you know that it was lamp-light, that the lamp was half turned down, and that you had no special reason to look hard at the case. It is quite possible that you may have overlooked the creature in the first instance.'

'No, no; it is out of the question.'

'And then Lee may have fallen into the river, and Norton been garrotted. It is certainly a formidable indictment that you have against Bellingham; but if you were to place it before a police magistrate, he would simply laugh in your face.'

'I know he would. That is why I mean to take the matter into my own hands.'

'Eh?'

'Yes; I feel that a public duty rests upon me, and besides, I must do it for my own safety, unless I choose to allow myself to be hunted by this beast out of the college, and that would be a little too feeble. I have quite made up my mind what I shall do. And first of all, may I use your paper and pens for an hour?'

'Most certainly. You will find all that you want upon that side-table.'

Abercrombie Smith sat down before a sheet of foolscap, and for an hour, and then for a second hour his pen travelled swiftly over it. Page after page was finished and tossed aside while his friend leaned back in his armchair, looking across at him with patient curiosity. At last, with an exclamation of satisfaction, Smith sprang to his feet, gathered his papers up into order, and laid the last one upon Peterson's desk.

'Kindly sign this as a witness,' he said.

'A witness? Of what?'

'Of my signature, and of the date. The date is the most important. Why, Peterson, my life might hang upon it.'

'My dear Smith, you are talking wildly. Let me beg you to go to bed.'

'On the contrary, I never spoke so deliberately in my life. And I will promise to go to bed the moment you have signed it.'

'But what is it?'

'It is a statement of all that I have been telling you to-night. I wish you to witness it.'

'Certainly,' said Peterson, signing his name under that of his companion. 'There you are! But what is the idea?'

'You will kindly retain it, and produce it in case I am arrested.'

'Arrested? For what?'

'For murder. It is quite on the cards. I wish to be ready for every event. There is only one course open to me, and I am determined to take it.'

'For Heaven's sake, don't do anything rash!'

'Believe me, it would be far more rash to adopt any other course. I hope that we won't need to bother you, but it will ease my mind to know that you have this statement of my motives. And now I am ready to take your advice and to go to roost, for I want to be at my best in the morning.'

Abercrombie Smith was not an entirely pleasant man to have as an enemy. Slow and easy-tempered, he was formidable when driven to action. He brought to every purpose in life the same deliberate resoluteness which had distinguished him as a scientific student. He had laid his studies aside for a day, but he intended that the day should not be wasted. Not a word did he say to his host as to his plans, but by nine o'clock he was well on his way to Oxford.

In the High Street he stopped at Clifford's, the gun-maker's, and bought a heavy revolver, with a box of central-fire cartridges. Six of them he slipped into the chambers, and half-cocking the weapon, placed it in the pocket of his coat. He then made his way to Hastie's rooms, where the big oarsman was lounging over his breakfast, with the *Sporting Times* propped up against the coffee-pot.

'Hullo! What's up?' he asked. 'Have some coffee?'

'No, thank you. I want you to come with me, Hastie, and do what I ask you.'

'Certainly, my boy.'

'And bring a heavy stick with you.'

'Hullo!' Hastie stared. 'Here's a hunting crop that would fell an ox.'

'One other thing. You have a box of

amputating knives. Give me the longest of them.'

'There you are. You seem to be fairly on the war trail. Anything else?'

'No; that will do.' Smith placed the knife inside his coat, and led the way to the quadrangle. 'We are neither of us chickens, Hastie,' said he. 'I think I can do this job alone, but I take you as a precaution. I am going to have a little talk with Bellingham. If I have only him to deal with, I won't, of course, need you. If I shout, however, up you come, and lam out with your whip as hard as you can lick. Do you understand?'

'All right. I'll come if I hear you bellow.'

'Stay here, then. I may be a little time, but don't budge until I come down.'

'I'm a fixture.'

Smith ascended the stairs, opened Bellingham's door and stepped in. Bellingham was seated behind his table, writing. Beside him, among his litter of strange possessions, towered the mummy case, with its sale number 249 still stuck upon its front, and its hideous occupant stiff and stark within it. Smith looked very deliberately round him, closed the door, and then, stepping across to the fireplace, struck a match and set the fire alight. Bellingham sat staring, with amazement and rage upon his bloated face.

'Well, really now, you make yourself at home,' he gasped.

Smith sat himself deliberately down, placing his watch upon the table, drew out his pistol, cocked it, and laid it in his lap. Then he took the long amputating knife from his bosom, and threw it down in front of Bellingham.

'Now, then,' said he, 'just get to work and cut up that mummy.'

'Oh, is that it?' said Bellingham with a sneer.

'Yes, that is it. They tell me that the law can't touch you. But I have a law that will set matters straight. If in five minutes you have not set to work, I swear by the God who made me that I will put a bullet through your brain!'

'You would murder me?'

Bellingham had half-risen, and his face was the colour of putty.

'Yes.'

'And for what?'

'To stop your mischief. One minute has gone.'

'But what have I done?'

'I know and you know.'

'This is mere bullying.'

'Two minutes are gone.'

'But you must give reasons. You are a

madman — a dangerous madman. Why should I destroy my own property? It is a valuable mummy.'

'You must cut it up, and you must burn it.'

'I will do no such thing.'

'Four minutes are gone.'

Smith took up the pistol and he looked towards Bellingham with an inexorable face. As the second-hand stole round, he raised his hand, and the finger twitched upon the trigger.

'There! there! I'll do it!' screamed Bellingham.

In frantic haste he caught up the knife and hacked at the figure of the mummy, ever glancing round to see the eye and the weapon of his terrible visitor bent upon him. The creature crackled and snapped under every stab of the keen blade. A thick, yellow dust rose up from it. Spices and dried essences rained down upon the floor. Suddenly, with a rending crack, its backbone snapped asunder, and it fell, a brown heap of sprawling limbs, upon the floor.

'Now into the fire!' said Smith.

The flames leaped and roared as the dried and tinder-like debris was piled upon it. The little room was like the stoke-hole of a steamer and the sweat ran down the faces of the two men; but still the one stooped and worked, while the other sat watching him with a set face. A thick, fat smoke oozed out from the fire, and a heavy smell of burned resin and singed hair filled the air. In a quarter of an hour a few charred and brittle sticks were all that was left of Lot No. 249.

'Perhaps that will satisfy you,' snarled Bellingham, with hate and fear in his little grey eyes as he glanced back at his tormentor.

'No; I must make a clean sweep of all your materials. We must have no more devil's tricks. In with all these leaves! They may have something to do with it.'

'And what now?' asked Bellingham, when the leaves also had been added to the blaze.

'Now the roll of papyrus which you had on the table that night. It is in that drawer, I think.'

'No, no,' shouted Bellingham. 'Don't burn that! Why, man, you don't know what you do. It is unique; it contains wisdom which is nowhere else to be found.'

'Out with it!'

'But look here, Smith, you can't really mean it. I'll share the knowledge with you. I'll teach you all that is in it. Or, stay, let me only copy it before you burn it!'

Smith stepped forward and turned the key in the drawer. Taking out the yellow, curled roll of paper, he threw it into the fire, and pressed it down with his heel. Bellingham screamed, and grabbed at it; but Smith pushed him back and stood over it until it was reduced to a formless, grey ash.

'Now, Master B.,' said he, 'I think I have pretty well drawn your teeth. You'll hear from me again, if you return to your old tricks. And now good morning, for I must go back to my studies.'

And such is the narrative of Abercrombie Smith as to the singular events which occurred in Old College, Oxford, in the spring of '84. As Bellingham left the university immediately afterwards, and was last heard of in the Soudan, there is no one who can contradict his statement. But the wisdom of men is small, and the ways of Nature are strange, and who shall put a bound to the dark things which may be found by those who seek for them?

A TOUGH TUSSLE

Ambrose Bierce

One night in the autumn of 1861 a man sat alone in the heart of a forest in western Virginia. The region was one of the wildest on the continent — the Cheat Mountain country. There was no lack of people close at hand, however; within a mile of where the man sat was the now silent camp of a whole Federal brigade. Somewhere about — it might be still nearer — was a force of the enemy, the numbers unknown. It was this uncertainty as to its numbers and position that accounted for the man's presence in that lonely spot; he was a young officer of a Federal infantry regiment and his business there was to guard his sleeping comrades in the camp against a surprise. He was in command of a detachment of men constituting a picket-guard. These men he had stationed just at nightfall in an irregular line, determined by the nature of the ground, several hundred yards in front of where he now sat. The line ran through the forest, among the rocks and laurel thickets, the men fifteen or twenty paces apart, all in concealment and under injunction of strict silence and unremitting vigilance. In four hours, if nothing occurred, they would be relieved by a fresh detachment from the reserve now resting in care of its captain some distance away to the left and rear. Before stationing his men the young officer of whom we are writing had pointed out to his two sergeants the spot at which he would be found if it should be necessary to consult him, or if his presence at the front line should be required.

It was a quiet enough spot — the fork of an old wood-road, on the two branches of which, prolonging themselves deviously forward in the dim moonlight, the sergeants were themselves stationed, a few paces in rear of the line. If driven sharply back by a sudden onset of the enemy — and pickets are not expected to make a stand after firing — the men would come into the converging roads and naturally following them to their point of intersection could be rallied and 'formed.' In his small way the author of these dispositions was something of a strategist; if Napoleon had planned as intelligently at Waterloo he would have won that memorable battle and been overthrown later.

Second-Lieutenant Brainerd Byring was a brave and efficient officer, young and comparatively inexperienced as he was in the business of killing his fellow-men. He had enlisted in the very first days of the war as a private, with no military knowledge whatever, had been made first-sergeant of his company on account of his education and engaging manner, and had been lucky enough to lose his captain by a Confederate bullet; in the resulting promotions he had gained a commission. He had been in several engagements, such as they were — at Philippi, Rich Mountain, Carrick's Ford and Greenbrier — and had borne himself with such gallantry as not to attract the attention of his superior officers. The exhilaration of battle was agreeable to him, but the sight of the dead, with their clay faces, blank eyes and stiff bodies, which when not unnaturally shrunken were unnaturally swollen, had always intolerably affected him. He felt toward them a kind of reasonless antipathy that was something more than the physical and spiritual repugnance common to us all. Doubtless this feeling was due to his unusually acute sensibilities — his keen sense of the beautiful, which these hideous things outraged. Whatever may have been the cause, he could not look upon a dead body without a loathing which had in it an element of resentment. What others have respected as the dignity of death had to him no existence — was altogether unthinkable. Death was a thing to be hated. It was not picturesque, it had no tender and solemn side — a dismal thing, hideous in all its manifestations and suggestions. Lieutenant Byring was a braver man than anybody knew, for nobody knew his horror of that which he was ever ready to incur.

Having posted his men, instructed his sergeants and retired to his station, he seated himself on a log, and with senses all alert began his vigil. For greater ease he loosened his sword-belt and taking his heavy revolver from his holster laid it on the log beside him. He felt very comfortable, though he hardly gave the fact a thought, so intently did he listen for any sound from the front which might have a menacing significance — a shout, a shot, or the footfall of one of his sergeants coming to apprise him of something worth knowing. From the vast, invisible ocean of moonlight overhead fell, here and there, a slender, broken stream that seemed to plash against the intercepting branches and trickle to earth, forming small white pools among the clumps of laurel. But these leaks were few and served only to accentuate the blackness of his environment, which his imagination found it easy to people with all manner of unfamiliar shapes, menacing, uncanny, or merely grotesque.

He to whom the portentous conspiracy of night and solitude and silence in the heart of a great forest is not an unknown experience needs not to be told what another world it all is — how even the most commonplace and familiar objects take on another character. The trees group themselves differently; they draw closer together, as if in fear. The very silence has another quality than the silence of the day. And it is full of half-heard whispers — whispers that startle — ghosts of sounds long dead. There are living sounds, too, such as are never heard under other conditions: notes of strange night-birds, the cries of small animals in sudden encounters with stealthy foes or in their dreams, a rustling in the dead leaves — it may be the leap of a wood-rat, it may be the footfall of a panther. What caused the breaking of that twig? — what the low, alarmed twittering in that bushful of birds? There are sounds without a name, forms without substance, translations in space of objects which have not been seen to move, movements wherein nothing is observed to change its place. Ah, children of the sunlight and the gaslight, how little you know of the world in which you live!

Surrounded at a little distance by armed and watchful friends, Byring felt utterly alone. Yielding himself to the solemn and mysterious spirit of the time and place, he had forgotten the nature of his connection with the visible and audible aspects and phases of the night. The forest was boundless; men and the habitations of men did not exist. The universe was one primeval mystery of darkness, without form and void, himself the sole, dumb questioner of its eternal secret. Absorbed in thoughts born of this mood, he suffered the time to slip away unnoted. Meantime the infrequent patches of white light lying amongst the tree-trunks had undergone changes of size, form and place. In one of them near by, just at the roadside, his eye fell upon an object that he had not previously observed. It was almost before his face as he sat; he could have sworn that it had not before been there. It was partly covered in shadow, but he could see that it was a human figure. Instinctively he adjusted the clasp of his sword-belt and laid hold of his pistol — again he was in a world of war, by occupation an assassin.

The figure did not move. Rising, pistol in hand, he approached. The figure lay upon its back, its upper part in shadow, but standing above it and looking down upon the face, he saw that it was a dead body. He shuddered and turned from it with a feeling of sickness and disgust, resumed his seat upon the log, and forgetting military prudence struck a match and lit a cigar. In the sudden blackness that followed the extinction of the flame he felt a sense of relief; he could no longer see the object of his aversion. Nevertheless, he kept his eyes set in that direction until it appeared again with growing distinctness. It seemed to have moved a trifle nearer.

'Damn the thing!' he muttered. 'What does it want?'

It did not appear to be in need of anything but a soul.

Byring turned away his eyes and began humming a tune, but he broke off in the middle of a bar and looked at the dead body. Its presence annoyed him, though he could hardly have had a quieter neighbor. He was conscious, too, of a vague, indefinable feeling that was new to him. It was not fear, but rather a sense of the supernatural — in which he did not at all believe.

'I have inherited it,' he said to himself. 'I suppose it will require a thousand ages — perhaps ten thousand — for humanity to outgrow this feeling. Where and when did it originate? Away back, probably, in what is called the cradle of the human race — the plains of Central Asia. What we inherit as a superstition our barbarous ancestors must have held as a reasonable conviction.

Doubtless they believed themselves justified by facts whose nature we cannot even conjecture in thinking a dead body a malign thing endowed with some strange power of mischief, with perhaps a will and a purpose to exert it. Possibly they had some awful form of religion of which that was one of the chief doctrines, sedulously taught by their priesthood, as ours teach the immortality of the soul. As the Aryans moved slowly on, to and through the Caucasus passes, and spread over Europe, new conditions of life must have resulted in the formulation of new religions. The old belief in the malevolence of the dead body was lost from the creeds and even perished from tradition, but it left its heritage of terror, which is transmitted from generation to generation — is as much a part of us as are our blood and bones.'

In following out his thought he had forgotten that which suggested it; but now his eye fell again upon the corpse. The shadow had now altogether uncovered it. He saw the sharp profile, the chin in the air, the whole face, ghastly white in the moonlight. The clothing was gray, the uniform of a Confederate soldier. The coat and waistcoat, unbuttoned, had fallen away on each side, exposing the white shirt. The chest seemed unnaturally prominent, but the abdomen had sunk in, leaving a sharp projection at the line of the lower ribs. The arms were extended, the left knee was thrust upward. The whole posture impressed Byring as having been studied with a view to the horrible.

'Bah!' he exclaimed; 'he was an actor — he knows how to be dead.'

He drew away his eyes, directing them resolutely along one of the roads leading to the front, and resumed his philosophizing where he had left off.

'It may be that our Central Asian ancestors had not the custom of burial. In that case it is easy to understand their fear of the dead, who really were a menace and an evil. They bred pestilences. Children were taught to avoid the places where they lay, and to run away if by inadvertence they came near a corpse. I think, indeed, I'd better go away from this chap.'

He half rose to do so, then remembered that he had told his men in front and the officer in the rear who was to relieve him that he could at any time be found at that spot. It was a matter of pride, too. If he abandoned his post he feared they would think he feared the corpse. He was no coward and he was unwilling to incur anybody's ridicule. So he again seated himself, and to prove his courage looked boldly at the body. The right arm

— the one farthest from him — was now in shadow. He could barely see the hand which, he had before observed, lay at the root of a clump of laurel. There had been no change, a fact which gave him a certain comfort, he could not have said why. He did not at once remove his eyes; that which we do not wish to see has a strange fascination, sometimes irresistible. Of the woman who covers her eyes with her hands and looks between the fingers let it be said that the wits have dealt with her not altogether justly.

Byring suddenly became conscious of a pain in his right hand. He withdrew his eyes from his enemy and looked at it. He was grasping the hilt of his drawn sword so tightly that it hurt him. He observed, too, that he was leaning forward in a strained attitude — crouching like a gladiator ready to spring at the throat of an antagonist. His teeth were clenched and he was breathing hard. This matter was soon set right, and as his muscles relaxed and he drew a long breath he felt keenly enough the ludicrousness of the incident. It affected him to laughter. Heavens! what sound was that? what mindless devil was uttering an unholy glee in mockery of human merriment? He sprang to his feet and looked about him, not recognizing his own laugh.

He could no longer conceal from himself

the horrible fact of his cowardice; he was thoroughly frightened! He would have run from the spot, but his legs refused their office; they gave way beneath him and he sat again upon the log, violently trembling. His face was wet, his whole body bathed in a chill perspiration. He could not even cry out. Distinctly he heard behind him a stealthy tread, as of some wild animal, and dared not look over his shoulder. Had the soulless living joined forces with the soulless dead? — was it an animal? Ah, if he could but be assured of that! But by no effort of will could he now unfix his gaze from the face of the dead man.

I repeat that Lieutenant Byring was a brave and intelligent man. But what would you have? Shall a man cope, single-handed, with so monstrous an alliance as that of night and solitude and silence and the dead, — while an incalculable host of his own ancestors shriek into the ear of his spirit their coward counsel, sing their doleful death-songs in his heart, and disarm his very blood of all its iron? The odds are too great — courage was not made for so rough use as that.

One sole conviction now had the man in possession: that the body had moved. It lay nearer to the edge of its plot of light — there could be no doubt of it. It had also moved its arms, for, look, they are both in the shadow!

A breath of cold air struck Byring full in the face; the boughs of trees above him stirred and moaned. A strongly defined shadow passed across the face of the dead, left it luminous, passed back upon it and left it half obscured. The horrible thing was visibly moving! At that moment a single shot rang out upon the picket-line — a lonelier and louder, though more distant, shot than ever had been heard by mortal ear! It broke the spell of that enchanted man; it slew the silence and the solitude, dispersed the hindering host from Central Asia and released his modern manhood. With a cry like that of some great bird pouncing upon its prey he sprang forward, hot-hearted for action!

Shot after shot now came from the front. There were shoutings and confusion, hoof-beats and desultory cheers. Away to the rear, in the sleeping camp, were a singing of bugles and grumble of drums. Pushing through the thickets on either side the roads came the Federal pickets, in full retreat, firing backward at random as they ran. A straggling group that had followed back one of the roads, as instructed, suddenly sprang away into the bushes as half a hundred horsemen thundered by them, striking wildly with their sabres as they passed. At headlong speed these mounted madmen shot past the spot where Byring had sat, and vanished round an angle of the road, shouting and firing their pistols. A moment later there was a roar of musketry, followed by dropping shots — they had encountered the reserve-guard in line; and back they came in dire confusion, with here and there an empty saddle and many a maddened horse, bullet-stung, snorting and plunging with pain. It was all over — 'an affair of outposts.'

The line was reestablished with fresh men, the roll called, the stragglers were reformed. The Federal commander with a part of his staff, imperfectly clad, appeared upon the scene, asked a few questions, looked exceedingly wise and retired. After standing at arms for an hour the brigade in camp 'swore a prayer or two' and went to bed.

Early the next morning a fatigue-party, commanded by a captain and accompanied by a surgeon, searched the ground for dead and wounded. At the fork of the road, a little to one side, they found two bodies lying close together — that of a Federal officer and that of a Confederate private. The officer had died of a sword-thrust through the heart, but not, apparently, until he had inflicted upon his enemy no fewer than five dreadful wounds. The dead officer lay on his face in a pool of blood, the weapon still in his breast. They turned him on his back and the surgeon removed it.

'Gad!' said the captain — 'It is Byring!' — adding, with a glance at the other, 'They had a tough tussle.'

The surgeon was examining the sword. It was that of a line officer of Federal infantry — exactly like the one worn by the captain. It was, in fact, Byring's own. The only other weapon discovered was an undischarged revolver in the dead officer's belt.

The surgeon laid down the sword and approached the other body. It was frightfully gashed and stabbed, but there was no blood. He took hold of the left foot and tried to straighten the leg. In the effort the body was displaced. The dead do not wish to be moved — it protested with a faint, sickening odor. Where it had lain were a few maggots, manifesting an imbecile activity.

The surgeon looked at the captain. The captain looked at the surgeon.

LADY WISHAW'S HAND

Richard Marsh

1

I

It was a woman's hand. In life, in its proper place at the end of a woman's arm, I could easily believe that it had been beautiful. But as it lay before me on the table, amidst the heap of papers in which it had been wrapped, I am bound to say that it was not its beauty that struck me first of all. One peculiar feature about it was its extraordinary state of preservation. Some embalming process must have been employed with which I was wholly unacquainted. It looked as if it were alive. Not only so. When, after some not inconsiderable amount of hesitation, I ventured to pick it up, it felt warm to the touch. Almost unwittingly, I pressed it — as I might have pressed a friendly hand in greeting. It seemed to return my pressure. Of course, it was all imagination. But it was imagination of rather a ghastly kind. So vivid was the delusion that I let it fall back on the table with a start that was sufficiently real.

The hand had been severed, with what had evidently been some sharp instrument, just above the wrist. A joint or some fraction of the bone — I am no anatomist — had apparently been withdrawn, so that the skin overlapped at the end. A white skin it was. I never saw a whiter. Yet it was not a bloodless white. Indeed, it was not difficult to believe that the warm blood was circulating underneath. It was a little hand. It struck me as being exquisitely shaped. A dainty hand. The fingers were long and slender, and tapered to a point. The finger-nails were perfect. They were pink, as are the finger-nails of some young girls. It was those almond-shaped, pink, well-kept finger-nails, which, as much as anything else gave to the hand such a curious semblance of life. The fingers and thumb were close together, so that as it lay palm downwards, the thumb was in the air, and only the finger-tips pressing against the table, the whole hand forming a sort of arch. It was a right hand. On the fore finger was a ring — so quaint a ring that, in itself, it was a curio. It was of plain gold, clumsily fashioned, and at the back it had been beaten out by some unskilled craftsman, into what had probably been intended to represent a heart-shaped shield. On it were some roughly graven words, which, at any rate, without a microscope, I was unable to decipher. I attributed the ring at a rough and ready estimate to perhaps the latter portion of the fourteenth century. It seemed odd to see that ill-shaped and ancient gewgaw on the pretty finger of that dainty little hand.

It was an extraordinary legacy, even for a collector to receive. It appeared that it *was* a legacy — this woman's hand. From a man, too, who had been but a shadowy acquaintance. It had reached me by a singularly matter-of-fact route — the parcels post. I wondered if the post-office officials would have said anything if they had known what it was that they were carrying. With it had come a letter, in which David Wishaw informed me that his brother, Colin, was dead, of which fact I had known nothing, and cared is possible still less; and that it had been one of Colin's very last requests that the hand which, according to David, had been known in the family as 'Lady Wishaw's hand' was a curiosity that I should value. Had he indeed! Kinder still, and kinder! The hand, said David, had been an heirloom in the family. Then what on earth did the man mean by passing his family heirlooms on to me, an almost utter stranger? It had been in the family, in uninterrupted sequence, since 1382. When I read that, I wondered whether the man took me for an idiot. The hand — that hand which was lying before me on the table — had not been in his family, or anybody's family, since 1382! I doubted very much if it had not been upon a living woman's arm, certainly within the last six months.

What was I to do with such a legacy? I might be a collector of curiosities, a virtuoso, or a bric-a-brac hunter, if you please. But I was not a curator of an anatomical museum. The curiosities which I collected did not include detached portions of the human frame. The Messrs Colin and David Wishaw seemed both of them to have laboured under the same misapprehension. I knew a man who collected the ropes with which criminals had been hung. He was a virtuoso of a kind which I was not. Mr Colin Wishaw should have bequeathed and Mr David Wishaw should have despatched — by means of the parcels post — this curiosity to him.

The ring on the finger did seem more in my way. Getting a magnifying glass, I endeavoured to make out the legend which was on the shield. The ring was old — there could be no doubt of that. It might date from 1382. The legend in the first place had been ill-done, and in course of time it had become so worn that even with the aid of a good glass, it was difficult to render.

' 'I take myne owne', that's what it is,' I

finally decided. 'It's either 'seke' or 'take'. I fancy it's 'take' — I take myne owne. I wonder if that is the motto of the Wishaws? I have a good mind to write to Mr David Wishaw, and to send him back the hand, and to tell him that, with his permission, as a mark of appreciation of his brother's thought for me, I'll keep the ring. I might add that, in my judgment, it would be as well if the hand were decently interred. — Let's see if I can take the ring off the lady's finger, so that I can have a look at it at closer quarters.'

With this idea and with the intention of putting the idea into execution, I once more picked up the hand — though I own I touched it with reluctance. Holding it with my left hand, grasping the ring with the fingers of my right, I prepared to work it loose. Instantly the hand shot up! It was clenched into a fist! I do not think I ever was so startled in my life. The action was so natural, so lifelike, that, though I was in my own drawing-room, and it was broad day, and there was no one present but the hand and myself, it seemed almost as if my heart had leapt into my mouth. It was no optical delusion — the open hand had become a tightened fist. No doubt it was owing to some muscular contraction — but it was muscular contraction of a sort I did not like. So startled was I that for some moments I did nothing else but stare. When I could do something else I dropped the hand as if it had been a red-hot coal. I sprang to my feet.

'I'll send it back to Mr David Wishaw, directly after lunch, ring and all!'

I was momentarily expecting lunch to be announced. It would not do to leave the hand lying on the table. So I hurriedly caught up the papers in which it had come, and, wrapping them about it anyhow, I put it in a cabinet which stood upon a small side-table.

As I was finishing lunch, there came a knock at the hall door. Nalder went to see who it was. Nalder is a most excellent servant; one whom scarcely anything would induce to forget his place. Therefore, I was the more surprised, when, after a few minutes' absence, he re-appeared with an expression of countenance which suggested both bewilderment and pain. He was rubbing his thigh, too, in a manner which, considering that he was standing in the presence of his master, was highly unbecoming.

'What's the matter, Nalder?'

'Well, sir, it's Mr Brasher, sir.'

'Mr Brasher? — What do you mean? — What's the matter with Mr Brasher?'

'Well, sir — nothing's the matter with Mr Brasher, that I am aware of, but — a most extraordinary thing has happened. At least, I beg your pardon, sir, it seems to me a most extraordinary thing. When I showed Mr Brasher up into the drawing-room, I noticed that the ormolu-cabinet which stands on the Chippendale tripod table, was open.' (This was the cabinet in which I had placed Mr Colin Wishaw's legacy. I must, unintentionally, have omitted to close it when I left the room.) 'I went to close it, and directly I had done so, just as I was turning round, someone or something caught me in the fleshy part of the leg, and gave me such a nip, that, I do believe, there's a piece nipped out.'

'Someone or something? What do you mean by someone or something?'

'I don't know, sir, I really don't. There was no one or nothing near me that I could see, and that's why I say it's a most extraordinary thing. But I never did feel anything so painful — never.'

I left Nalder still rubbing his thigh in a manner which his previous conduct had certainly given me no reason to expect from him. When I went upstairs, I found Martin Brasher standing in the centre of the room with a look on his face which might have been twin brother to the look I had seen on Nalder's.

'Pugh,' was his salutation to me as I went

in, 'what on earth have you got in this room of yours?'

'I have a good many things in this room of mine, as, if you had eyes, you would be able to see. What is the matter with you?'

'Upon my word, I hardly know what is the matter with me. Do you know, I was just sitting on that armchair, waiting for you, when something — it felt like somebody's finger-nails — scratched my cheek from top to bottom. Isn't there a scratch to be seen?'

There was, unmistakably. On his left cheek there was what was, obviously, the mark of a recent scratch.

'You've been in dreamland, Brasher, and scratched yourself in your dream.'

'Nothing of the kind. I tell you what — Pugh, it's uncommonly queer! But never mind about that now; I have come to tell you that I've got a case at last.'

'A case of what?'

'A case for the Society — a genuine ghost. Have you ever heard of a man named Wishaw?' (I had very much indeed, and very recently. But he didn't give me a chance. He was so very full of his subject that he went dashing on, without noticing that he had not afforded me an opportunity to answer.) 'They're a Scotch family, the Wishaws — one of those Scotch families which antedate the

Deluge. They've had some peculiar characters among them in their time, more peculiar than pleasant — as some of these Scotch families have had a way of having. One of the most peculiar was a woman, who lived somewhere about the close of the fourteenth century — a propitious period, especially in Scotland, for peculiar characters. She is known amongst them to this day, as 'Lady Wishaw'. You know how they have that sort of thing in stories. She was the most beautiful woman that ever was — that's of course. She was, also, the wickedest woman that ever was — that's equally of course. She does appear to have done something to deserve a niche, as the latter, in the temple of fame. She was a thief. Such a thief that she became notorious as a thief, even in that age and land of thieves. She stole from foes and friends alike. At last, in the house of a friend, she was caught, red-handed, in some more astounding theft than usual. We should have called her a kleptomaniac, I suspect, in these later days. The term was not invented then, nor the thing. To her host she appeared to have been guilty of an act of hideous treachery. Taking upon himself, as was not uncommon, in those sweet and simple days, the offices of judge, jury and executioner, there and then he hacked off her hand at the wrist. The first intimation which the Wishaws received of the latest *petit faux pas* in which the lady had indulged, came to them in rather grisly fashion. The lady's guilty but, I understand, lovely member was sent to them by the host in charge of a special messenger. The lady herself they never saw again — at least, in life. She felt, when she had lost her hand, that she had lost all that there was worth living for. She destroyed herself within the hour. Thus, as you perceive, there was ample ground why a pleasant little feud should exist, henceforth, between the whilom friends, the Wishaws and the Macfies; — the host's name was, it seems, Macfie.

'The story goes that the dismembered lady managed to convey some sort of spiritual intimation to her relatives, to the effect that they were never to cease from killing while a Macfie still remained to cumber the ground. Thenceforward, the first end and aim of the Wishaws was to kill the Macfies. And in order that they might not forget their high calling, a special injunction was laid on them that they were to keep the hacked-off hand ever with them as a sort of heirloom, and as a perpetual reminder, until the last of the Macfies was slain. Not only so. They were given clearly to understand, that should a Wishaw arise, who, before the Macfies were wholly exterminated, should prove unworthy, and should cease from killing, the dead hand would turn against the living man, and would measure out to him that measure which he should have measured out to the Macfies.

'This is a queer story.' (I felt that it was.) 'But the queerest part is still to come. I am informed, on credible authority, that the hand was never embalmed. That nothing had been done to preserve it, of any sort or kind. That it has continued, uninterruptedly, in the possession of the Wishaws. And that, after the passage of the centuries, it still looks as fresh and as lifelike as if its original owner still had it in the proper place at the end of her arm.'

As to the truth of this portion of his story, touching the appearance of life which the hand possessed, I could have gone to the cabinet, taken out its contents and given him the proof on the spot; and I may add, that I should have done it, had it not been that a contraction of the muscles of my throat seemed to keep me a fixture in my chair.

'Pugh, I mean to see that hand.' He should have seen it, then and there, had not the sensation of which I had suddenly become conscious almost amounted to strangulation. 'It strikes me that there's a clear case for the Psychical Research Society at last. I have chanced, almost by accident, upon some extraordinary stories of Lady Wishaw's hand. It seems that the Wishaws did keep on killing the Macfies. But the latter was a prolific breed. As soon as a sire was struck down a son sprang up. There came a time when murder, even in Scotland, was not looked upon with such lenient eyes. Still the Wishaws pursued the even tenour of their way. More than one of them has brought himself within the clutches, and has suffered the last penalties of the law. Finally, even the Wishaws succumbed to the influence of the new spirit of the newer age. They declined to keep on murdering. In fact, they ceased to murder. When they ceased, the hand — the dead hand — Lady Wishaw's hand, began. Pugh — I have reason to believe that, literally, for generations, the head of the family for the time being, has been found strangled in his bed.'

Brasher paused. He stood in front of me, with a dramatic gesture. With an effort, I found myself able to speak.

'Where did you get that piece of information from, may I enquire?'

'Never mind where I got it from; it is so. You may take it from me that the thing was kept hushed up. It was given out that they died from a spasmodic affection of the heart. Nothing of the kind. There never yet was a

Wishaw with a weak heart. At last, only two of them were left, Colin Wishaw, the head of the house, and David, his younger brother. Colin was something like a madman. From the little I had seen of him, he had struck me as being about as mad as a man could be, without being pronounced, legally and medically, insane. He swore a great oath that he would rid himself, and the family, of Lady Wishaw's hand.'

'If what you have told me is correct, Brasher, I fail to see any signs of madness in his doing that.'

'The extraordinary part of the thing was the way in which he set himself to carry out his oath. He put the hand in a coffin, and buried it, coffin and all. Lady Wishaw's hand returned to him from the grave.'

'Oh, Brasher, come!'

'So I am told. He took it with him across the Atlantic. In mid-ocean he dropped it into the sea. When he reached his hotel in New York he found it at his bedside in the morning. He cast it into a smelter's furnace. It was waiting for him when he got home. I am credibly assured that he cooked it, and ate it, only to find it on his pillow when he went to bed.'

'Brasher, your story begins to remind me of a poem which I read in my childhood days, which, if I remember rightly was called, and appropriately called, 'A Horrible Tale'.'

'Wait a bit. About a fortnight ago Colin Wishaw was found dead in his bed. There was no mistake about it this time — he had been strangled. It was impossible to hush it up. An inquest was held. The verdict was, that he had been strangled by some person or persons unknown.'

If that were so, what on earth did David Wishaw mean by saying that, almost with his last breath, Colin had bequeathed, what appeared to be, *par excellence*, the heirloom of the Wishaws, as a legacy to me. Mr David Wishaw was a nice man, upon my word!

'The present possessor of Lady Wishaw's hand,' continued Brasher, 'is David Wishaw, the last living representative of the Wishaw strain.'

Was he? He would very soon be the possessor, though he was not then.

'I am going to call on Mr David Wishaw. I shall request him to allow me to examine the hand. I intend to make enquiries as to the truth of its extraordinary history. As I have told you, I have reason to believe that its truth will be made quite plain; should that be so, I shall present the case for the immediate consideration of the Psychical Research Society. I think you will agree with me that a more remarkable case will hardly come its way.'

I quite agreed that, if — that little 'if' — he could find evidence to prove it, it would be a remarkable case. And I was more than once on the point of informing him that, if he really desired to look at and to examine Lady Wishaw's hand, he need go no further than where he stood. But each time, as the words had already almost escaped my lips, I again became conscious of that I can only describe as that curious, and distinctly involuntary suppression of the larynx.

II

When Martin Brasher went, he left, so to speak, his story behind him. I heartily wished he had not. The story might sound incredible. It might, even, sound absurd. But there are men, sane men, who are entirely of opinion that it is quite within the bounds of reason to suppose that there may be, what the world commonly calls, spiritual manifestations — dealings between the seen and the unseen. Of such men I avowedly am one. And the idea that there had come to me, from such a death bed as Colin Wishaw's appeared to have been, a gift, which was, in itself, a ghastly gift, and with which was associated such a history — the mere idea, to me, was full of horror.

Besides, what had prevented me from speaking? What was it that had caused that sensation of pressure about the region of my throat, and so stayed me from telling Brasher that the thing for which he was about to seek, all the time, was at his side, within reach of his arm? What had pinched Nalder? It was a ridiculous inquiry, perhaps — but what had? What had scratched Brasher's face? What had caused the open hand to shut up into a clenched fist, before my very eyes? Was it because the hand, though dead, was living, and was still attached to a living form, though unseen?

Men are made in different fashions. Some men would have found in my situation, nothing but pleasurable excitement. For my part I sat in my chair and perspired. I was unwilling to be left alone in my own drawing-room, even though it was broad day. Nothing but shame prevented me from summoning Nalder to come and keep me company.

On one point I was resolved, that Lady Wishaw's hand should not remain in my possession. For two hours I endeavoured to summon up sufficient resolution to enable me to rise from my chair, and to go to the cabinet, and to take out the hand, and to pack it up, and to return it from whence it came. As I look back upon those two hours, I am half inclined to wonder how it was, that, as they have it in the nightmare stories, during their passage, my hair did not turn grey. All the while I had the consciousness that something was in the room with me. Something seemed to keep stroking the back of my hand — something with the delicate touch of a dainty woman. I knew that the starch was coming out of my linen. I felt that my collar was becoming as limp as a rag. At last, with what, positively, amounted to a frenzied effort, I sprang from my seat, rushed to the cabinet, opened it, and reached out for the hand, and found that it was not there!

There could be no question as to what were the effects of being endowed with too vivid an imagination — in the papers in which I had hastily wrapped Lady Wishaw's hand, before going down to lunch, there was nothing at all.

'Nalder! Nalder!'

I scarcely think that I expected him to hear me call. I am under the impression that I hardly spoke above a whisper. I began to stagger toward the door, intending to go out on to the landing and call him loudly. As I turned, something was placed against my mouth. Something which felt like the slender fingers of a woman's hand. And my lips were sealed!

2

I dined at the club. I am unable to say how I reached it. I know that I did reach it. For me, at least, that is sufficient. I had a little table at the third window from the door.

Perkins was my waiter. Perkins is not only an excellent waiter; he is, what is almost of as much importance, an excellent man. I am persuaded that Perkins and I have many things in common. He knows exactly what I like and how I like it. When he tells me what to eat, I eat it, without so much as a hint of an amendment. Never yet have I found that the house of my confidence has been builded on the sand.

I remember that on that particular night, I had one of the finest woodcocks I ever tasted. Plain roast. I almost incline to believe that Perkins must have raised that bird himself, have shot it himself, have hung it himself, and have cooked it himself, he had its history so completely at his finger-ends. Brasher's story, and my two hours' agony, had almost faded from my mind. I do not say that the woodcock was wholly responsible, but it had certainly borne its part. I was just going to drink my second glass of champagne — I don't care what anybody says, everybody has his own taste, and with woodcock I like champagne. I daresay, in another half minute, I should have thanked God that I was alive. The glass was still on its way to my lips when, without any sort of a warning, in an instant there returned to me that hideous consciousness which had been with me in the afternoon, that something was in the room. I do not meant the waiters, or the diners, and that sort of thing. I wish I did. I mean something intangible, unseen.

I put down my glass, untasted. A cold shiver went over me. Then I began to perspire. My feeling was one of the acutest misery. My first impulse, in spite of the woodcock, was to wish that I was dead. In that brilliantly lighted room, with all the people about me, I was afraid. Perkins was at my side. He had his back to me, for some cause or other, at the moment. All at once he faced round to me with quite a little twirl. To be frank it was not the kind of movement which was becoming to Perkins. One of his great charms is, that he never evinces what I consider indecorous signs of haste. Of an actual twirl, as if he had been a sort of human teetotum, I do not think that he had ever been guilty before.

'I beg your pardon, sir?'

I have no doubt that I looked at him with what were lack-lustre eyes. I believed that I murmured, 'Eh?'

'Did you touch me, sir?'

'Touch you? What do you mean?'

'I really must ask you to excuse, sir,' — Perkins is an educated man — 'but I certainly was under the impression, sir, that you pulled my coat-tails.'

I pulled his coat-tails! A waiter's! I had, after all, over estimated Perkins' intellectual powers, if he could suppose that I could be capable of such an action as that. But I said nothing. I rose from the table there and then, and went away. I daresay that Perkins imagined that I was bitterly offended. I should certainly have been justified in being so. Or, perhaps, he imagined that I had suddenly gone mad. I left my second glass of champagne untasted. I did not wait for the sweets — Perkins has an exquisite taste in sweets. His sweets never give me indigestion. I said nothing about his wife. (I always inquire after Perkins' wife, who I understand is paralysed, and as good as dead — when he has seen that I have had a creditable dinner.) I went into the smoking-room. I do not know why. I was in no mood to smoke. I take it that I went there simply because, with that intangible unseen something keeping me company, I could not go home.

Several men were in the smoking-room. Tolerably comfortable they seemed, as for a moment I stood at the door and looked round. I envied them. Their contentment with the position in life in which they found themselves placed was so transparently greater than mine. My moving to a seat seemed to create a slight sensation. Each man, as I passed him, gave a perceptible start. Again, I don't know why — I had scarcely seated myself before I became aware that something curious was going on. I seemed to have brought with me an element of discord into the room. Those that had seemed so wholly at their ease, as I viewed them from the door, seemed, all at once, to have been attacked by a fit of the fidgets. A most pronounced type of the fidgets, too. The attack seemed to be passing, from one smoker to the other, right round the room. Under cover of an evening paper I pretended to notice nothing. But I did. Man after man sprang up in his seat, and looked about him with an air of startled surprise. Pranklyn was sitting in front of me. 'Plain' Pranklyn, they call him, to distinguish him from the other Pranklyn — 'Picture' Pranklyn — who has a chamber of horrors which he calls his picture gallery. Plain Pranklyn is in his seventies, and would turn the scale I daresay, at eighteen stone. So when I say that suddenly he sprang up from his seat, as if he had been an india rubber ball, I am aware that the language which I use is strong.

'Good God!' he exclaimed.

Everybody looked at him. All the room was in a stir.

'What is up, Pranklyn?' asked Sir Gerald Carr.

'Who was that caught hold of my hand?'

'Caught hold of your hand? What do you mean?'

'Hanged if I know what I do mean.' Pranklyn looked to me, as if he were on the verge of an apoplectic fit. 'I know that someone caught hold of my hand and twisted it right round.'

A man whom I didn't know spoke next.

'That's odd. A moment before someone, or something, did exactly the same thing to me.'

'By George!' cried old Jack Brett. 'But there's the devil in the room. I'll swear that someone nearly pulled me hand clean off me wrist.'

'And mine!' 'And mine!'

Nearly every person present claimed to have undergone a similar experience. There were a score of men turning the smoking-room into a bedlam. I don't know what the committee would have said. I, for my part, sat as if I were glued to the chair. For, directly Pranklyn sprang from his seat, I felt a hand steal into mine, and fingers and a thumb clasp it about.

'Hullo,' said Carr, 'what's gone wrong with you? You don't look well.'

I rose from my seat with a palsied start. As I did so, the hand let go.

'I'm not feeling well. I — I think that I'll go home.' I went home, there and then. As I moved across the room, every man jack of them followed me with their eyes. I didn't know if they thought that I had bewitched them, or played some hanky-panky trick. They looked as if they did.

As I went along the passage, and down the steps into the street, I felt someone twitching at my coat sleeve. I hailed a cab. I bade the cabman drive me home. All the time, as he drove me through the streets, I felt as if there were someone seated beside me in the cab; someone who constantly twitched me by the arm. I doubt if there was ever a sane creature in such a state of mind as I then was. Nalder let me in. He started when he saw my face.

'I hope, sir, you are not ill?'

'To tell the truth, Nalder, I'm not feeling quite the thing. I think I'll have some brandy in my bedroom, and go to bed.'

I had the strangest reluctance to go, unaccompanied, up my own staircase. I hung about in the hall until Nalder appeared with some brandy on a tray. Together we went up, he in front, and I behind. I don't know what he thought of me. He is too well trained a servant to betray his feelings in his face. At the same time, he is possessed of too much discernment to have failed to see that my indisposition was of a peculiar kind, especially, when under one pretext and another, I kept him in my bedroom until I was actually between the sheets in bed.

'Shall I leave the light burning, sir?'

It is a peculiarity of mine that I never can sleep where there is a light in the room. On that occasion my choice seemed to lie between the devil and the deep sea. The idea of being left in the dark filled me with a paralysis of horror. On the other hand, what might I not be destined to witness, if the room was light. I chose, mechanically, what I could only hope would turn out to be the lesser evil of the two.

'Leave it burning. If I find that it keeps me from sleeping, I will get out of bed and put it out.'

I did not get out of bed to put it out. Queerly enough, scarcely had Nalder turned his back, than I fell asleep. I must have done because I remember nothing after he left the room. Nothing, that is, until I awoke. I was not troubled with a dream. I just have slept the quiet, dreamless sleep of tired childhood.

What woke me, I do not know, even to this hour. I know that I did wake, to find myself in a cold sweat of agony, quivering under the overwhelming burden of some unknown horror. For some moments, I was only conscious that the room was still lighted. At first, I seemed to have to gasp for breath. But, by degrees, the curtain of unconsciousness was partly lifted, and I became aware that something was with me in the room. Whatever it was, I cannot say. It was something too, which touched me on the brow, with a light touch, such as we might use to waken a sleeper out of sleep. Only that touch was like the touch of death. I believe that it *was* the touch of death. Light though it was, under it I could not move. While it remained, I doubt if I breathed. I lay, as I have said, in a cold sweat of agony. When the touch was removed, I closed my eyes. I was afraid of what it was I might see. For what was a period of a few moments, I suppose, nothing happened, though I never, for an instant, lost consciousness of the presence which was with me in the room. As I lay with my eyes fast closed, in agony, something

— something tangible — fell on my cheek from above. It had something of the effect of an electric shock. With what I apprehend was an involuntary tension of the muscles of my body, I leaped out of bed onto the floor. I believe that, as I stood on the floor, I cried. Then I stretched out my arms on either side of me, as a blind man might do. Then, and only then, I opened my eyes, and looked and saw. Leaning over the bed, I saw that, on the pillow on which my head had just been lying, was a ring.

I never had a moment's doubt as to the ring's identity. Having seen it once, it was one which I could never forget. It was the ring which had been on the fore-finger of the hand which, according to David Wishaw, his brother Colin had bequeathed me as a legacy. The ring which the dead hand had seemed to resent my attempting to remove from its place, by clenching itself into a fist. Was it possible that it was offered me as a present after all? Then, by whom? My heart melted within me, as I realised that it was an offering from the presence which was with me in the room.

I shrunk away. I extended my arms as if to prevent the ring from coming to closer quarters. As I did so I saw a hand advancing across the pillow from the opposite side of the bed. It was the hand which, having once been seen under such circumstances as I had seen it, was no more to be mistaken than the ring. It was, indeed, the hand to which it belonged. The hand of which Brasher had told such a horrible tale. The hand which according to him had urged to murder through the centuries, and then, when its urging had failed, had murdered on its own account.

I saw the hand coming slowly across the bed. It at no time touched the pillow, but, without any visible support, was in the air at a distance above the pillow, of, perhaps, a couple of inches. I saw the dainty fingers close upon the ring. When I saw that, with a spasmodic effort I turned my face away. My glance fell upon the clock which was on the mantelshelf. I noticed, with a singular degree of vividness, that according to that clock, the time was five and twenty minutes to four.

A touch came on my arm. I started round. In front of me was the hand. It was palm uppermost. On the open palm was the ring. It was being held out for me to take. But I would have none of it; although the chance of becoming the possessor of so genuine and unique a curio was hardly likely ever to me again in my way. I slunk back. The hand followed me. It moved quicker than I did. It caught me by the wrist. It pressed the ring against my palm. But still I would have none of it. I made no attempt to close my hand so as to retain the ring within my grasp.

Suddenly the something which guided and ruled the hand — never, as I have said, for a moment did I lack consciousness of the something which was there — suddenly this something seemed to become annoyed. My persistent, automatic refusal of the proffered ring seemed, in some fantastic way, to give annoyance. All at once, the hand was withdrawn. It was clenched. It was held before me in the air. I saw the ring between the little, dainty fingers. Then with an extraordinary degree of violence, it was thrown against my face.

3

'Why are you lying there upon the floor?'

It was Brasher's voice. I found, as he said, that I was lying in my night shirt on the floor. I sat up. I saw that the light still burned.

'Has it gone?'

'Has what gone? What has happened to your face?'

I put my hand up to my face. When I removed it, it was dabbled with blood. It all came back to me — the extreme violence of the movement with which the hand had hurled the ring at me through the air.

'The ring!' was all I said.

'The ring? What ring?' I rose to my feet. I dimly perceived that, for some cause, Brasher was almost as much disturbed as myself.

We looked each other in the face. 'Pugh!' He caught me by the arm. His hand was shaking. 'Where is Lady Wishaw's hand?'

I looked around the room. 'Is it still here?'

'Here? Where? For God's sake don't speak like that. Your voice is as hoarse as a crow's.'

I felt him shiver.

'Why did you not tell me, yesterday, that you were the present fortunate possessor of

Lady Wishaw's hand?'

I said nothing. He went on. Owing to his haste, or to some other cause, he seemed to pronounce his words as if he were temporarily afflicted with an impediment in his speech.

'It's been at its devil's tricks again. I've come straight from Wishaw's. David's dead.'

'Dead! — David Wishaw! — Brasher!'

'Don't look at me like that. You look at me as if you were looking at a ghost.' Taking out his handkerchief, he wiped his brow. 'Yes, David Wishaw's dead. He was the last of the breed. With him, all of them have gone. It seems that this morning, at a quarter after three — '

'When?'

'This morning, at a quarter after three, his servants heard him screaming in his room. When they went to his aid, they could not get to him, because the door was locked. They heard him fighting and yelling within. They called to him but could get no answer. All was still when the shrieking ceased. They found the door open. They found him dead. He had been strangled. He was a strong man. He must have fought furiously for his life, because they found him lying in a hideous heap on his bed.'

'Brasher, Lady Wishaw's hand was with me

here at five and twenty minutes to four.'

'Pugh!' His jaw dropped down.

'Yes, Brasher, it was here with me.'

'Are you sure that you are not mistaken?'

'And because I would not have the ring which it endeavoured to force on my acceptance, it flung it in my face, with such violence, that it cut my face right open, as you see. I wonder if that ring is anywhere upon the floor?'

No. We searched everywhere. But it was nowhere to be found. After all, the hand had vanished with that ancient gewgaw of a ring. Acting up to the legend which seemed to me to have been inscribed upon it, Lady Wishaw's hand had taken its own.

But if I had accepted it!

THE MARK OF THE BEAST

Rudyard Kipling

Your Gods and my Gods?
— do you or I know which is the stronger?
— Native Proverb

East of Suez, some hold, the direct control of Providence ceases; Man being there handed over to the power of the Gods and Devils of Asia, and the Church of England Providence only exercising an occasional and modified supervision in the case of Englishmen.

This theory accounts for some of the more unnecessary horrors of life in India: it may be stretched to explain my story.

My friend Strickland of the Police, who knows as much of natives of India as is good for any man, can bear witness to the facts of the case. Dumoise, our doctor, also saw what Strickland and I saw. The inference which he drew from the evidence was entirely incorrect. He is dead now; he died in a rather curious manner, which has been elsewhere described.

When Fleete came to India he owned a little money and some land in the Himalayas, near a place called Dharmsala. Both properties had been left him by an uncle, and he came out to finance them. He was a big, heavy, genial, and inoffensive man. His knowledge of natives was, of course, limited, and he complained of the difficulties of the language.

He rode in from his place in the hills to spend New Year in the station, and he stayed with Strickland. On New Year's Eve there was a big dinner at the club, and the night was excusably wet. When men foregather from the uttermost ends of the Empire they have a right to be riotous. The Frontier had sent down a contingent o' Catch-'em-Alive-O's who had not seen twenty white faces for a year, and were used to ride fifteen miles to dinner at the next Fort at the risk of a Khyberee bullet where their drinks should lie. They profited by their new security, for they tried to play pool with a curled-up hedgehog found in the garden, and one of them carried the marker round the room in his teeth. Half a dozen planters had come in from the south and were talking 'horse' to the Biggest Liar in Asia, who was trying to cap all their stories at once. Everybody was there, and there was a general closing up of ranks and taking stock of our losses in dead or disabled that had fallen during the past year. It was a very wet night, and I remember that we sang 'Auld Lang Syne' with our feet in the Polo Championship Cup, and our heads among the stars, and swore that we were all dear friends. Then some of us went away and annexed Burma, and some tried to open up the Soudan and were opened up by Fuzzies in that cruel scrub outside Suakim, and some found stars and medals, and some were married, which was bad, and some did other things which were worse, and the others of us stayed in our chains and strove to make money on insufficient experiences.

Fleete began the night with sherry and bitters, drank champagne steadily up to dessert, then raw, rasping Capri with all the strength of whisky, took Benedictine with his coffee, four or five whiskies and sodas to improve his pool strokes, beer and bones at half-past two, winding up with old brandy. Consequently, when he came out, at half-past three in the morning, into fourteen degrees of frost, he was very angry with his horse for coughing, and tried to leapfrog into the saddle. The horse broke away and went to his stables; so Strickland and I formed a Guard of Dishonour to take Fleete home.

Our road lay through the bazaar, close to a little temple of Hanuman, the Monkey-god, who is a leading divinity worthy of respect. All gods have good points, just as have all priests. Personally, I attach much importance to Hanuman, and am kind to his people — the great gray apes of the hills. One never knows when one may want a friend.

There was a light in the temple, and as we passed we could hear voices of men chanting hymns. In a native temple the priests rise at all hours of the night to do honour to their god. Before we could stop him, Fleete dashed up the steps, patted two priests on the back, and was gravely grinding the ashes of his cigar-butt in to the forehead of the red stone image of Hanuman. Strickland tried to drag him out, but he sat down and said solemnly:

'Shee that? Mark of the B — beasht! I made it. Ishn't it fine?'

In half a minute the temple was alive and noisy, and Strickland, who knew what came of polluting gods, said that things might occur. He, by virtue of his official position, long residence in the country, and weakness for going among the natives, was known to the priests and he felt unhappy. Fleete sat on the ground and refused to move. He said that 'good old Hanuman' made a very soft pillow.

Then, without any warning, a Silver Man came out of a recess behind the image of the god. He was perfectly naked in that bitter, bitter cold, and his body shone like frosted silver, for he was what the Bible calls 'a leper as white as snow.' Also he had no face, because he was a leper of some years' standing, and his disease was heavy upon him. We two stooped to haul Fleete up, and the temple was filling and filling with folk who seemed to spring from the earth, when the Silver Man ran in under our arms, making a noise exactly like the mewing of an otter, caught Fleete round the body and dropped his head on Fleete's breast before we could wrench him away. Then he retired to a corner and sat mewing while the crowd blocked all the doors.

The priests were very angry until the Silver Man touched Fleete. That nuzzling seemed to sober them.

At the end of a few minutes' silence one of the priests came to Strickland and said, in perfect English, 'Take your friend away. He has done with Hanuman but Hanuman has not done with him.' The crowd gave room and we carried Fleete into the road.

Strickland was very angry. He said that we might all three have been knifed, and that Fleete should thank his stars that he had escaped without injury.

Fleete thanked no one. He said that he wanted to go to bed. He was gorgeously drunk.

We moved on, Strickland silent and wrathful, until Fleete was taken with violent shivering fits and sweating. He said that the smells of the bazaar were overpowering, and he wondered why slaughter-houses were permitted so near English residences. 'Can't you smell the blood?' said Fleete.

We put him to bed at last, just as the dawn was breaking, and Strickland invited me to have another whisky and soda. While we were drinking he talked of the trouble in the temple, and admitted that it baffled him completely. Strickland hates being mystified by natives, because his business in life is to overmatch them with their own weapons. He has not yet succeeded in doing this, but in fifteen or twenty years he will have made some small progress.

'They should have mauled us,' he said, 'instead of mewing at us. I wonder what they meant. I don't like it one little bit.'

I said that the Managing Committee of the temple would in all probability bring a criminal action against us for insulting their religion. There was a section of the Indian Penal Code which exactly met Fleete's offence. Strickland said he only hoped and prayed that they would do this. Before I left I looked into Fleete's room, and saw him lying on his right side, scratching his left breast. Then I went to bed cold, depressed, and unhappy, at seven o'clock in the morning.

At one o'clock I rode over to Strickland's house to inquire after Fleete's head. I imagined that it would be a sore one. Fleete was breakfasting and seemed unwell. His temper was gone, for he was abusing the cook for not supplying him with an underdone chop. A man who can eat raw meat after a wet night is a curiosity. I told Fleete this and he laughed.

'You breed queer mosquitoes in these parts,' he said. 'I've been bitten to pieces, but only in one place.'

'Let's have a look at the bite,' said Strickland. 'It may have gone down since this morning.'

While the chops were being cooked, Fleete opened his shirt and showed us, just over his left breast, a mark, the perfect double of the black rosettes — the five or six irregular blotches arranged in a circle — on a leopard's hide. Strickland looked and said, 'It was only pink this morning. It's grown black now.'

Fleete ran to a glass.

'By Jove!' he said, 'this is nasty. What is it?'

We could not answer. Here the chops came in, all red and juicy, and Fleete bolted three in a most offensive manner. He ate on his right grinders only, and threw his head over his right shoulder as he snapped the meat. When he had finished, it struck him that he had been behaving strangely, for he said apologetically, 'I don't think I ever felt so hungry in my life. I've bolted like an ostrich.'

After breakfast Strickland said to me, 'Don't go. Stay here, and stay for the night.'

Seeing that my house was not three miles from Strickland's, this request was absurd. But Strickland insisted, and was going to say something, when Fleete interrupted by declaring in a shame-faced way that he felt hungry again. Strickland sent a man to my house to fetch over my bedding and a horse, and we three went down to Strickland's stables to pass the hours until it was time to go out for a ride. The man who has a weakness for horses never wearies of inspecting them; and when two men are killing time in this way they gather knowledge and lies the one from the other.

There were five horses in the stables, and I shall never forget the scene as we tried to look them over. They seemed to have gone mad. They reared and screamed and nearly tore up their pickets; they sweated and shivered and lathered and were distraught with fear. Strickland's horses used to know him as well as his dogs; which made the matter more curious. We left the stable for fear of the brutes throwing themselves in their panic. Then Strickland turned back and called me. The horses were still frightened, but they let us 'gentle' and make much of them, and put their heads in our bosoms.

'They aren't afraid of us,' said Strickland. 'D' you know, I'd give three months' pay if Outrage here could talk.'

But Outrage was dumb, and could only cuddle up to his master and blow out his nostrils, as is the custom of horses when they wish to explain things but can't. Fleete came up when we were in the stalls, and as soon as the horses saw him, their fright broke out afresh. It was all that we could do to escape from the place unkicked. Strickland said, 'They don't seem to love you, Fleete.'

'Nonsense,' said Fleete; 'my mare will follow me like a dog.' He went to her; she was in a loose-box; but as he slipped the bars she plunged, knocked him down, and broke away into the garden. I laughed, but Strickland was not amused. He took his moustache in both fists and pulled at it till it nearly came out. Fleete, instead of going off to chase his property, yawned, saying that he felt sleepy. He went to the house to lie down, which was a foolish way of spending New Year's Day.

Strickland sat with me in the stables and asked if I had noticed anything peculiar in Fleete's manner. I said that he ate his food like a beast; but that this might have been the result of living alone in the hills out of the reach of society as refined and elevating as ours for instance. Strickland was not amused.

I do not think that he listened to me, for his next sentence referred to the mark on Fleete's breast, and I said that it might have been caused by blister-flies, or that it was possibly a birth-mark newly born and now visible for the first time. We both agreed that it was unpleasant to look at, and Strickland found occasion to say that I was a fool.

'I can't tell you what I think now,' said he, 'because you would call me a madman; but you must stay with me for the next few days, if you can. I want you to watch Fleete, but don't tell me what you think till I have made up my mind.'

'But I am dining out to-night,' I said.

'So am I,' said Strickland, 'and so is Fleete. At least if he doesn't change his mind.'

We walked about the garden smoking, but saying nothing — because we were friends, and talking spoils good tobacco — till our pipes were out. Then we went to wake up Fleete. He was wide awake and fidgeting about his room.

'I say, I want some more chops,' he said. 'Can I get them?'

We laughed and said, 'Go and change. The ponies will be round in a minute.'

'All right,' said Fleete. 'I'll go when I get the chops — underdone ones, mind.'

He seemed to be quite in earnest. It was

four o'clock, and we had had breakfast at one; still, for a long time, he demanded those underdone chops. Then he changed into riding clothes and went out into the verandah. His pony — the mare had not been caught — would not let him come near. All three horses were unmanageable — mad with fear — and finally Fleete said that he would stay at home and get something to eat. Strickland and I rode out wondering. As we passed the temple of Hanuman the Silver Man came out and mewed at us.

'He is not one of the regular priests of the temple,' said Strickland. 'I think I should peculiarly like to lay my hands on him.'

There was no spring in our gallop on the racecourse that evening. The horses were stale, and moved as though they had been ridden out.

'The fright after breakfast has been too much for them,' said Strickland.

That was the only remark he made through the remainder of the ride. Once or twice, I think, he swore to himself; but that did not count.

We came back in the dark at seven o'clock, and saw that there were no lights in the bungalow. 'Careless ruffians my servants are!' said Strickland.

My horse reared at something on the

carriage drive, and Fleete stood up under its nose.

'What are you doing, grovelling about the garden?' said Strickland.

But both horses bolted and nearly threw us. We dismounted by the stables and returned to Fleete, who was on his hands and knees under the orange-bushes.

'What the devil's wrong with you?' said Strickland.

'Nothing, nothing in the world,' said Fleete, speaking very quickly and thickly. 'I've been gardening — botanising, you know. The smell of the earth is delightful. I think I'm going for a walk — a long walk — all night.'

Then I saw that there was something excessively out of order somewhere, and I said to Strickland, 'I am not dining out.'

'Bless you!' said Strickland. 'Here, Fleete, get up. You'll catch fever there. Come in to dinner and let's have the lamps lit. We'll all dine at home.'

Fleete stood up unwillingly, and said, 'No lamps — no lamps. It's much nicer here. Let's dine outside and have some more chops — lots of 'em and underdone — bloody ones with gristle.'

Now a December evening in Northern India is bitterly cold, and Fleete's suggestion was that of a maniac.

'Come in,' said Strickland sternly. 'Come in at once.'

Fleete came, and when the lamps were brought, we saw that he was literally plastered with dirt from head to foot. He must have been rolling in the garden. He shrank from the light and went to his room. His eyes were horrible to look at. There was a green light behind them, not in them, if you understand, and the man's lower lip hung down.

Strickland said, 'There is going to be trouble — big trouble — to-night. Don't you change your riding-things.'

We waited and waited for Fleete's reappearance, and ordered dinner in the meantime. We could hear him moving about his own room, but there was no light there. Presently from the room came the long-drawn howl of a wolf.

People write and talk lightly of blood running cold and hair standing up, and things of that kind. Both sensations are too horrible to be trifled with.

My heart stopped as though a knife had been driven through it, and Strickland turned as white as the tablecloth.

The howl was repeated, and was answered by another howl far across the fields.

That set the gilded roof on the horror. Strickland dashed into Fleete's room. I followed, and we saw Fleete getting out of the window. He made beast-noises in the back of his throat. He could not answer us when we shouted at him. He spat.

I don't quite remember what followed, but I think that Strickland must have stunned him with the long boot-jack, or else I should never have been able to sit on his chest. Fleete could not speak, he could only snarl, and his snarls were those of a wolf, not of a man. The human spirit must have been giving way all day and have died out with the twilight. We were dealing with a beast that had once been Fleete.

The affair was beyond any human and rational experience. I tried to say 'Hydrophobia,' but the word wouldn't come, because I knew that I was lying.

We bound this beast with leather thongs of the punkah-rope, and tied its thumbs and big toes together, and gagged it with a shoe-horn, which makes a very efficient gag if you know how to arrange it. Then we carried it into the dining-room, and sent a man to Dumoise, the doctor, telling him to come over at once. After we had despatched the messenger and were drawing breath, Strickland said, 'It's no good. This isn't any doctor's work.' I, also, knew that he spoke the truth.

The beast's head was free, and it threw it about from side to side. Any one entering the room would have believed that we were curing a wolf's pelt. That was the most loathsome accessory of all.

Strickland sat with his chin in the heel of his fist, watching the beast as it wriggled on the ground, but saying nothing. The shirt had been torn open in the scuffle and showed the black rosette mark on the left breast. It stood out like a blister.

In the silence of the watching we heard something without — mewing like a she-otter. We both rose to our feet, and, I answer for myself, not Strickland, felt sick — actually and physically sick. We told each other, as did the men in Pinafore, that it was the cat. Dumoise arrived, and I never saw a little man so unprofessionally shocked. He said that it was a heart-rending case of hydrophobia, and that nothing could be done. At least any palliative measures would only prolong the agony. The beast was foaming at the mouth. Fleete, as we told Dumoise, had been bitten by dogs once or twice. Any man who keeps half a dozen terriers must expect a nip now and again. Dumoise could offer no help. He could only certify that Fleete was dying of hydrophobia. The beast was then howling, for it had managed to spit out the shoe-horn. Dumoise said that he would be ready to certify to the cause of death, and that the end was certain. He was a good little man, and he offered to remain with us; but Strickland refused the kindness. He did not wish to poison Dumoise's New Year. He would only ask him not to give the real cause of Fleete's death to the public.

So Dumoise left, deeply agitated; and as soon as the noise of the cart-wheels had died away, Strickland told me, in a whisper, his suspicions. They were so wildly improbable that he dared not say them out aloud; and I, who entertained all Strickland's beliefs, was so ashamed of owning to them that I pretended to disbelieve.

'Even if the Silver Man had bewitched Fleete for polluting the image of Hanuman, the punishment could not have fallen so quickly.'

As I was whispering this the cry outside the house rose again, and the beast fell into a fresh paroxysm of struggling till we were afraid that the thongs that held it would give way.

'Watch!' said Strickland. 'If this happens six times I shall take the law into my own hands. I order you to help me.'

He went into his room and came out in a few minutes with the barrels of an old shotgun, a piece of fishing-line, some thick cord, and his heavy wooden bedstead. I reported that the convulsions had followed the cry by two seconds in each case, and the beast seemed perceptibly weaker.

Strickland muttered, 'But he can't take away the life! He can't take away the life!'

I said, though I knew that I was arguing against myself, 'It may be a cat. It must be a cat. If the Silver Man is responsible, why does he dare to come here?'

Strickland arranged the wood on the hearth, put the gun-barrels into the glow of the fire, spread the twine on the table, and broke a walking stick in two. There was one yard of fishing line, gut lapped with wire, such as is used for mahseer-fishing, and he tied the two ends together in a loop.

Then he said, 'How can we catch him? He must be taken alive and unhurt.'

I said that we must trust in Providence, and go out softly with polo-sticks into the shrubbery at the front of the house. The man or animal that made the cry was evidently moving round the house as regularly as a night-watchman. We could wait in the bushes till he came by and knock him over.

Strickland accepted this suggestion, and we slipped out from a bath-room window into the front verandah and then across the carriage drive into the bushes.

In the moonlight we could see the leper

coming round the corner of the house. He was perfectly naked, and from time to time he mewed and stopped to dance with his shadow. It was an unattractive sight, and thinking of poor Fleete, brought to such degradation by so foul a creature, I put away all my doubts and resolved to help Strickland from the heated gun-barrels to the loop of twine — from the loins to the head and back again — with all tortures that might be needful.

The leper halted in the front porch for a moment and we jumped out on him with the sticks. He was wonderfully strong, and we were afraid that he might escape or be fatally injured before we caught him. We had an idea that lepers were frail creatures, but this proved to be incorrect. Strickland knocked his legs from under him and I put my foot on his neck. He mewed hideously, and even through my riding-boots I could feel that his flesh was not the flesh of a clean man.

He struck at us with his hand and feet-stumps. We looped the lash of a dog-whip round him, under the arm-pits, and dragged him backwards into the hall and so into the dining-room where the beast lay. There we tied him with trunk-straps. He made no attempt to escape, but mewed.

When we confronted him with the beast

the scene was beyond description. The beast doubled backwards into a bow as though he had been poisoned with strychnine, and moaned in the most pitiable fashion. Several other things happened also, but they cannot be put down here.

'I think I was right,' said Strickland. 'Now we will ask him to cure this case.'

But the leper only mewed. Strickland wrapped a towel round his hand and took the gun-barrels out of the fire. I put the half of the broken walking stick through the loop of fishing-line and buckled the leper comfortably to Strickland's bedstead. I understood then how men and women and little children can endure to see a witch burnt alive; for the beast was moaning on the floor, and though the Silver Man had no face, you could see horrible feelings passing through the slab that took its place, exactly as waves of heat play across red-hot iron — gun-barrels for instance.

Strickland shaded his eyes with his hands for a moment and we got to work. This part is not to be printed.

The dawn was beginning to break when the leper spoke. His mewings had not been satisfactory up to that point. The beast had fainted from exhaustion and the house was very still. We unstrapped the leper and told him to take away the evil spirit. He crawled to the beast and laid his hand upon the left breast. That was all. Then he fell face down and whined, drawing in his breath as he did so.

We watched the face of the beast, and saw the soul of Fleete coming back into the eyes. Then a sweat broke out on the forehead and the eyes — they were human eyes — closed. We waited for an hour, but Fleete still slept. We carried him to his room and bade the leper go, giving him the bedstead, and the sheet on the bedstead to cover his nakedness, the gloves and the towels with which we had touched him, and the whip that had been hooked round his body. He put the sheet about him and went out into the early morning without speaking or mewing.

Strickland wiped his face and sat down. A night-gong, far away in the city, made seven o'clock.

'Exactly four-and-twenty hours!' said Strickland. 'And I've done enough to ensure my dismissal from the service, besides permanent quarters in a lunatic asylum. Do you believe that we are awake?'

The red-hot gun-barrel had fallen on the floor and was singeing the carpet. The smell was entirely real.

That morning at eleven we two together went to wake up Fleete. We looked and saw that the black leopard-rosette on his chest had disappeared. He was very drowsy and tired, but as soon as he saw us, he said, 'Oh! Confound you fellows. Happy New Year to you. Never mix your liquors. I'm nearly dead.'

'Thanks for your kindness, but you're over time,' said Strickland. 'To-day is the morning of the second. You've slept the clock round with a vengeance.'

The door opened, and little Dumoise put his head in. He had come on foot, and fancied that we were laying out Fleete.

'I've brought a nurse,' said Dumoise. 'I suppose that she can come in for . . . what is necessary.'

'By all means,' said Fleete cheerily, sitting up in bed. 'Bring on your nurses.'

Dumoise was dumb. Strickland led him out and explained that there must have been a mistake in the diagnosis. Dumoise remained dumb and left the house hastily. He considered that his professional reputation had been injured, and was inclined to make a personal matter of the recovery. Strickland went out too. When he came back, he said that he had been to call on the Temple of Hanuman to offer redress for the pollution of the god, and had been solemnly assured that no white man had ever touched the idol, and that he was an incarnation of all the virtues labouring under a delusion. 'What do you think?' said Strickland.

I said, 'There are more things . . . '

But Strickland hates that quotation. He says that I have worn it threadbare.

One other curious thing happened which frightened me as much as anything in all the night's work. When Fleete was dressed he came into the dining-room and sniffed. He had a quaint trick of moving his nose when he sniffed. 'Horrid doggy smell, here,' said he. 'You should really keep those terriers of yours in better order. Try sulphur, Strick.'

But Strickland did not answer. He caught hold of the back of a chair, and, without warning, went into an amazing fit of hysterics. It is terrible to see a strong man overtaken with hysteria. Then it struck me that we had fought for Fleete's soul with the Silver Man in that room, and had disgraced ourselves as Englishmen for ever, and I laughed and gasped and gurgled just as shamefully as Strickland, while Fleete thought that we had both gone mad. We never told him what we had done.

Some years later, when Strickland had married and was a church-going member of society for his wife's sake, we reviewed the incident dispassionately, and Strickland suggested that I should put it before the public.

I cannot myself see that this step is likely to clear up the mystery; because, in the first place, no one will believe a rather unpleasant story, and, in the second, it is well known to every right-minded man that the gods of the heathen are stone and brass, and any attempt to deal with them otherwise is justly condemned.

We do hope that you have enjoyed reading this large print book.

Did you know that all of our titles are available for purchase?

We publish a wide range of high quality large print books including:
Romances, Mysteries, Classics
General Fiction
Non Fiction and Westerns

Special interest titles available in large print are:
The Little Oxford Dictionary
Music Book
Song Book
Hymn Book
Service Book

Also available from us courtesy of Oxford University Press:
Young Readers' Dictionary
(large print edition)
Young Readers' Thesaurus
(large print edition)

For further information or a free brochure, please contact us at:
Ulverscroft Large Print Books Ltd.,
The Green, Bradgate Road, Anstey,
Leicester, LE7 7FU, England.
Tel: (00 44) **0116 236 4325**
Fax: (00 44) **0116 234 0205**

RUDYARD … born in Bombay in December … from England in the autumn of 18… his seventeenth birthday, to work as a … first on the *Civil and Military Gazette* in Lahore, then on the *Pioneer* at Allahabad. The poems and stories he wrote over the next seven years laid the foundation of his literary reputation, and soon after his return to London in 1889 he found himself world-famous. Throughout his life his works enjoyed great acclaim and popularity, but he came to seem increasingly controversial because of his political opinions, and it has been difficult to reach literary judgements unclouded by partisan feeling. This series, published half a century after Kipling's death, provides the opportunity for reconsidering his remarkable achievement.

LOUIS L. CORNELL has taught English literature and philology at Dartmouth College and Columbia University. The author of *Kipling in India*, he is an independent scholar living in Manhattan.